An Illegal Solution

They made a good team, perhaps because their characters were so different: Detective-Sergeant O'Connor lived for tomorrow, Detective-Constable Brent only for today. O'Connor was a family man, Brent took his pleasures where he found them. So when the incidence of drug-related crimes showed a disturbing rise, their reactions to the fact were not at all the same: while Brent merely regretted it, O'Connor saw it as a direct threat to all the things in life he most valued, and believed he was called upon to take whatever measures were necessary to counter such a threat. It was a mistake that was to lead to an act of folly which put his career on the line. And when Brent, with typical, carefree indifference to the consequences, rushed in to help, he ran head first into murderous danger and not just his career but his life was at stake.

JEFFREY ASHFORD

An Illegal Solution

COLLINS, 8 GRAFTON STREET, LONDON W1

William Collins Sons & Co. Ltd
London · Glasgow · Sydney · Auckland
Toronto · Johannesburg

First published 1990
© Jeffrey Ashford 1990

British Library Cataloguing in Publication Data

Ashford, Jeffrey
  An illegal solution.—(Crime Club)
  I. Title
  823.914[F]

ISBN 0 00 232312 5

Photoset in Linotron Baskerville by
Rowland Phototypesetting Ltd
Bury St Edmunds, Suffolk
Printed in Great Britain by
William Collins Sons & Co. Ltd, Glasgow

CHAPTER 1

Detective-Inspector Fawcus was a man who believed that his subordinates should respect but not like him; to be liked was proof that one was not working others hard enough. He fiddled with his lower lip as he stared at the large-scale map of Seetonhurst which hung on the wall. 'The meeting's at this end house in Fairview Crescent, which is up for sale and empty?'

'That's right,' replied Detective-Sergeant O'Connor, a tall man whose height was masked by a slight stoop and who looked older than he was because his face was heavily lined and his expression was so often serious. 'But we've no time. All my informant can say is it will be after dark.'

'And the middle-aged man with a scar on his cheek will be there; but there's still no hint of his identity? Not exactly a mine of information, your man.'

'It is a lead,' replied O'Connor defensively.

'Which needs to be a damned sight better than the last one, which cost us a full team out on the streets for six hours and a no-show. Unless, of course, the targets slipped through unseen.'

It was not the first time the DI had suggested that five nights previously the members of the surveillance team had not kept an efficient watch. O'Connor, a man of firm loyalties, said: 'There's no way that could have happened.'

'Of course not,' replied the DI ironically. He turned away from the map and sat behind the desk. 'All right. Set it up.'

O'Connor, back in his room which was next to the DI's, picked up a pencil, ready to write out the names of the surveillance team for that night; but then he just stared into space. The police relied, perhaps more than they ever willingly admitted, on information from criminals. But, because this was given by men for whom truth and honesty were strange words, inevitably there were times when the information given turned out to be totally wrong or even a hoax. He did not believe that either possibility had been the case five days previously or that it might be now. Nevertheless . . .

He was a worrier, but a parochial one. He worried about his family and his job, but not about ozone holes. He believed that it was a policeman's job to ensure that there was justice, not necessarily that the clear-up rate looked good—a belief that often did not endear him to his superiors. He feared drugs and loathed those who dealt in them even more than did most parents because he so often had to deal with the victims. He knew that a good home and loving parents were no guarantee that a youngster would not turn, or be turned, to drug-taking. He could name many addicts who had come from happy backgrounds. More than once, he'd counselled his own children—Harry was fourteen, Liz was twelve—about the perils of drugs and he hoped they'd accepted what he'd said, but he knew only too well that in the flush of youth, a danger could be seen as a spur . . .

By God, how he hoped that this second tip-off proved to be more fruitful than the first! So far, they hadn't a single lead into the new drugs mob who were becoming very active in the area . . .

He jerked his mind back to the present and began to write out the names of the surveillance team. Brent . . .

Brent turned round on the travelling rug and stared across the field at Susan, who stood on the edge of a cleft in the hill. The sharp sunshine filled her auburn hair with extra colour and from time to time the slight breeze moulded her frock against her shapely body. At that distance, he could not see her deep blue eyes, the upturned tip of her nose, or the rich curves of her full lips, but he could visualize them.

He turned on his back and closed his eyes. Six months previously she'd witnessed a traffic accident and it had been his job to take a statement from her at the station. He was a handsome, rugged, outdoor, touch of the when-men-were-men type (not his judgement; that of many women he'd known), but she had treated him with a cold politeness that almost, but never quite, spilled into disdain. Unable to resist the challenge, he'd thought up an excuse to visit her home. A large Georgian house set in its own grounds, five miles from Seetonhurst. The setting had in no way awed him. He might not be his bank's favourite client, but he knew he was every bit as good as the next person. At this second meeting, that supercilious indifference with which the rich protected their inner selves had been even more in evidence. He'd written her off as not worth the effort.

A few days later she'd telephoned the station. It was, she had said, just possible that she had mistakenly given him some incorrect information so he'd better call at the house the next day. Not so indifferent to his charms as she'd tried to make out, he told himself. He'd made the mistake of allowing his confidence to show. Her manner had cooled a few degrees even from the arctic temperature at which it had been previously operating. Forgetting Rule No. 14 in the *Conduct, Manners, and Ethics Manual*, he had become overtly rude. She had smiled. A smile that left him puzzled for the rest of the day.

During the next fortnight, he'd twice decided to telephone her, twice had checked himself. She was used to homage and therefore if she failed to receive it, she would be intrigued. (It was convenient to forget that it must have been obvious that he was not indifferent.) Fifteen days later she had telephoned to say, in a bored voice, that if he liked watching polo, she was going to a match in which some of her friends were playing. He'd answered that he'd far prefer to watch a game of darts at the local. It appeared that that was something she'd always wanted to see.

They'd sparred through several meetings. Insults had been freely exchanged and personal habits criticized. A casual eavesdropper might have thought they disliked each other, especially when his hands began wandering and she had asked him if it really was necessary to behave like a thirteen-year-old trying to discover sex. Such casual eavesdropper would have realized his mistake one Wednesday afternoon when it had been she who had suggested they went back to her place because her parents were staying with friends and the daily was away, suffering from one of her dizzy spells . . .

Now she strolled back across the springy weed grass, avoiding a patch of brambles, and came to a stop just short of the rug. 'What are you so deep in thought about?' She sat, her movements filled with grace.

'I was wondering why it took me so long to fall in love with you; all of twenty-four hours?'

'Remind me to kiss you to help you find out.' She did not—as another woman might—reach out to hold his hand in a quick gesture of returning love. She neither showed, nor welcomed, the slightest display of affection in public.

He looked away from her and out, beyond the edge of the hill, at the countryside four hundred feet below. Seetonhurst was hidden, so what were visible were fields, woods, an occasional house, and, six miles away, the town of Bradington, too indistinct to be ugly. Three generations back, his paternal ancestors had been farmers and presumably it was from them that he had inherited a love of the country. If ever he won the pools, he'd buy an Elizabethan manor house with sufficient stabling for her to keep half a dozen horses . . .

'Let's move.' She stood.

She became easily bored, lacking his ability to let time slide effortlessly past. She had not suffered his training— hours spent watching and waiting and only imagination and memories to keep boredom at bay. He folded up the travelling rug and followed her uphill to the small parking area by the road. She climbed into the Escort, carelessly slammed the door shut. She owned a Porsche 911 Turbo and naturally far preferred to drive around in that, but he insisted on the Escort when they went out together. The house was hers, so the car had to be his.

Grangeway, a large detached house with a generous garden both to the front and back, had been built twenty years before. He'd never been certain why she owned it since she'd never previously lived in it or let it, but from something she'd once said, he'd gained the impression that it possibly represented the product of a tax fiddle on the part of her father. Christopher Radford, was smooth, hard, and clever.

He shut the front door and turned to carry the rug over to the hall cupboard. 'Leave that and come on upstairs,' she said. 'I'm hungry.'

Initially, he'd been surprised and, absurdly, embarrassed by the way in which she often demanded that they made love during the day. He thought of himself as thoroughly modern, but his upbringing had inculcated in him certain tenets which he found himself unable to ignore and one of these was that sex, always at the initiative of the male, did not take place until after dark.

They went up the stairs and along a corridor to the end bedroom. She liked him to undress her, slowly and with a show of reluctance. Indifference, perhaps because she so often used it as a weapon, excited her. Stripped, she was more perfectly formed than any woman had a right to be . . .

The phone rang.

'Forget it,' she murmured.

He picked up the receiver. O'Connor said: 'Where the hell have you been? I've been trying to contact you all day. Get on down here double sharp.'

'Look, it's my day off—'

'It was.' The line went dead.

He replaced the receiver. 'The sarge is shouting for me.'

'Let him bloody shout.'

'Something really sharp must have turned up. I'm sorry, but we'll just have to speed things up.'

'One word from him and it's wham, bam, and not even a thank you, ma'am?'

'I said, I'm sorry . . .'

'Don't give it a second thought. You must observe your priorities.' She swivelled round, stood, began to dress.

CHAPTER 2

The surveillance team had been split into three units; two were in cars, the third in a house owned by a man who had been in the police force before his retirement and who had given the police permission to use his place as an observation post.

Time spent in a room in the dark, staring out at a street in which nothing happened, went slowly. PC Eastern said complainingly: 'I'm missing my favourite programme on the telly.'

'You're too young to know what I'm missing,' replied Brent.

'This is the second surveillance job I've been lumbered with in a week . . . I need a drag. Is it all right if I slip outside for a fag?'

'Kill yourself if you want.' Brent continued to stare through the gap between the lace curtains at the end house on the other side of the road, missing nothing but his mind elsewhere. When he returned to Grangeway, in what sort of a mood was he going to find Susan? Everything had always come so easily to her that she became furious if events didn't go exactly as she wanted . . .

A car, slowing right down, came into view. He whistled.

Eastern hurried into the room and stubbed out the cigarette in an ashtray. The car turned off the road to drive up to the garage of the penultimate house. In the headlights, they saw a woman climb out and go round the bonnet to unlock the garage doors. 'False alarm,' said Brent.

'You've made me waste a fag,' complained Eastern. He returned to the chair in which he'd previously been sitting, checked the time. 'Are they ever going to show?'

The DI had earlier nicked himself shaving that morning and there was a trace of blood on the left side of his square jaw; a conservative man in all things, he always used a safety razor and never an electric one. He leaned back in his chair. 'So?'

'It was a blank,' replied O'Connor wearily.

'What I'm asking is, why?'

'Duff info, a change of plan . . .' He shrugged his shoulders.

'Or a leak?'

'No.'

'This is the second no-show.'

'A leak's impossible. I didn't name the target area until half an hour before the off.'

'It doesn't take half an hour to make a phone call.'

'There's no traitor here.'

'That's something we're going to have to find out.'

'If you think . . .'

'It's happened before and inevitably it'll happen again.'

'Not in my outfit it won't.'

'You'd better remember that pride goes before a fall.'

O'Connor's lips tightened. It was not pride in his own capabilities which made him convinced that none of those who served under him could ever be a traitor, but pride in such subordinates.

'Get back on to your informant and find out what went

wrong.' The DI spoke more easily. 'I'll grant one thing. If they were all like you, it would be impossible.'

O'Connor was only slightly mollified.

He returned to his own room, sat, and stared at the small framed photograph on the right of the desk. Pam and the two kids, taken some years back so that Liz had gappy teeth and Harry still had a trace of the angelic look which boys possessed before they began to sup at life. It had to be an exaggeration to hold that right now he was battling to secure the safety of their future, but that was how he felt. And his failure to succeed had resulted in suspicion being thrown on the CID and those from the uniform branch who had been on the last two operations. He knew that there had been traitors in the force in the past, and there would be others in the future, but he simply refused to acept that any of 'his' men could prove to be one such . . .

He hated every criminal, no matter how minor his crime, because ripples of hurt spread out to injure the innocent. But he hated these as yet unknown drug-dealers with a far greater passion because they threatened both people and ideals.

In the space of a few days, several drug-related incidents involving under-eighteens were reported.

Five boys, all around fifteen, were caught in the lavatories of the Hugh Merton Comprehensive School with crack that they were nerving themselves to try.

The senior inspector of a society funded by voluntary contributions identified a girl of fourteen who was prostituting herself to pay for her recently acquired drug addiction.

Two seventeen-year-olds mainlined with badly contaminated heroin and escaped death only because the hospital to which they were rushed had had previous experience in similar cases.

Several of those at a teenagers' party held in a house in the smart north-west suburb of Alonsby experimented with snorting cocaine and one of them proved to be allergic to the adulterant and suffered a reaction so violent that he died in the ambulance.

In addition to these young victims, there were many others, older, who suffered the direct and indirect effects of their own or others' addictions . . .

The external phone rang and O'Connor picked up the receiver.

'It's me, Guv.'

He recognized the hoarse voice immediately. 'What the hell happened?' He pictured Wallace. Round face, nervous mouth, flabby body; someone who crept around in the shadows, fearing to expose himself to the sunlight.

'You near got me throat slashed, that's what happened. They saw a split near the house and reckoned they'd been grassed and started looking for the grasser.'

O'Connor knew a tremendous sense of relief. There was no traitor among the police, only a detective or a PC who'd become careless. 'Have they sussed you?'

'Wouldn't be talking now, would I, if they'd managed?'

'Do they still think they may have been grassed?'

'Don't seem that way.'

One of the factors in the police's favour was the instinct of people at risk to reject, if possible, a conclusion that would be unwelcome. They'd decided that the policeman's presence in or near Fairview Crescent had been a coincidence. 'So what's going to happen?'

'You think I'm saying after you lot bleeding well near had me buried?'

'It won't happen again,' said O'Connor soothingly. 'He'll have been a youngster out on his first surveillance job. I'll identify him and see he's sent back to routine.'

'I don't know nothing.'

'You know quite a lot because you're smart.'

'It's because I'm smart that I don't know nothing. Give

you names and you'll move and this time they'll know someone's talking. Maybe they'll bloody well find me.'

'I can arrange it so that they don't suss a thing.'

'Like last time?'

'It can't happen again . . . I can find a couple of centuries for hard info.'

There was no immediate response, but O'Connor waited with confident patience. Grassers grassed for many reasons and often, as now, for more than one. Wallace needed the money, but, a weak man, he also needed the sense of power which came from an act of betrayal.

Wallace finally said: 'Seems like there's another meeting being set up on account of the last being a bust.'

'When and where?'

'I can't say.'

'You'll need to, to make the two centuries.'

'I'll be back.' The line went dead.

O'Connor replaced the receiver, drummed with his fingers on the desk, stood and left to go next door. The room was empty, but as he turned away he saw the DI round the corner at the far end of the corridor, his athletic strides quickly taking him past a civilian typist.

The DI passed O'Connor and sat behind his desk. He looked up. 'For the past half-hour I've had to suffer local civic dignitaries expressing their deep concern over the growing incidence of crime and wondering if we're aware of what's going on. So unless you've come with good news, keep your mouth tight shut and clear off.'

'There wasn't a leak in the Fairview Crescent op. It went sour because one of our lads broke cover and was sussed by the villains.'

The DI leaned back in the chair. 'That's the best possible news.' He'd originally voiced his suspicions not because he was any less proud than O'Connor of the force and those who served in it, but because he was more cynical about human nature.

'I'll try and identify who it was and blast his ears off him . . . My informant reckons another meeting's being set up to take the place of the one that went sour.'

'When and where?'

'For the moment he's not saying. He's scared because the mob started looking for a grasser and although they've quietened down now, if anything fires them up again, he thinks they might nail him.'

'Wave a few quid under his nose—that'll check such morbid thoughts.'

'I've offered him a couple of centuries for some hard information.'

'Two hundred!' The DI's voice rose. 'Where in hell d'you expect to find that sort of money?'

'Can't you put in a special requisition, citing the expressed concern of the local bigwigs?'

'That would have to be accompanied by an assurance that information vital to a case and unobtainable by any other means will be forthcoming if the requisition is granted. Can you give me such an assurance?'

'Yes, provided you don't expect me to support it with facts.'

CHAPTER 3

From the settee, Susan said: 'I want a cognac.'

Brent, about to sit, looked across the sitting-room. 'We finished the bottle the other evening.'

'I bought another this morning.'

He was annoyed. The agreement was that he bought the food and the drink.

'Surely you don't begrudge my giving us a little present?'

He didn't reply because any answer would probably make him sound ridiculous. A man living with a woman far wealthier than he was always at risk—if he complained when she bought things he couldn't afford, he was being small-minded and perverse; if he didn't complain, he was showing that he was willing to live off her.

He went through to the larder beyond the large and very well equipped kitchen. On one of the shelves was an unopened bottle of Rémy Martin, VSOP. He carried this through to the cocktail cabinet in the sitting-room, poured out two drinks, handed her one of the balloon glasses.

'Am I forgiven?' she asked.

He didn't need to see the gleam in her eyes to know she was mocking him. He sat.

'You know I told you before you left this morning that I was having lunch at Mereton? Afterwards, I had a long chat with Chris.' She called her parents by their Christian names; a habit he still found odd. 'About you.'

'What was the point at issue? Whether he'd come after me with a horsewhip or, perhaps more appropriately, a dog whip?'

She laughed. 'Always a hundred years behind the times! Nowadays unmarried daughters' despoilers are no longer socially *de trop*. Anyway, Chris is very broad-minded. So long as I'm happy, he's happy.'

'And what does your mother feel about us?'

'The real question is, does she feel? I'm never quite certain what the answer to that is. Sometimes I think she merely operates on delayed reflexes . . . Chris asked what you intended to do in life.'

'Can't he accept that I'm a humble policeman?'

'You're far too intelligent to dream of remaining one.'

'On the principle that police work doesn't call for intelligence?'

'Climb off your high horse. You need a job with a decent salary. Chris has offered to find you a place with one of his companies. It'll have to be a fairly low one to start with, of course, but he reckons from what he's seen of you that it'll not take you long to begin climbing.'

'Using the backs of people who've far more experience and ability, but aren't friendly with the boss's daughter?'

'So what? Only a fool doesn't seize his advantages.'

'No allowance for ideals?'

'Ideals mature as income rises.'

'Can't you believe in anything?'

'I believe that a comfortable life is a hell of a lot more fun than an uncomfortable one . . . Be a sweet and refill my glass.'

The phone rang.

'The meeting's on Friday,' said Wallace, his hoarse voice pitched so low that it was only just audible.

'Where's it to be and who'll be there?' asked O'Connor.

'I don't know nothing more until I see the folding.'

'Where d'you want to meet?'

'Six tomorrow evening at Loton Green station.'

'Why's it have to be that far away?'

'Because I don't aim to end up like Lofty.'

'Lofty who?'

'And you call yourself a split!' The connection was cut.

O'Connor scratched a two-day-old mosquito bite which still irritated. Presumably somebody mixed up in the drug racket had recently suffered. But no Lofty had turned up as a victim in G Division. He telephoned county HQ and spoke to the duty divisional liaison officer.

'Lofty rings a bell, Sarge, but I can't say why off the top of my head. Hang on and I'll skim through the weekly divisional crime reports.'

He waited.

'Six days ago Frank Randall, nickname Lofty because he makes five foot five when he's wearing high heels, was picked up off a building site in Newford. The latest hospital report says he may live, but not to bet better than evens on it.'

'He was badly beaten up?'

'Heavily sanded down. They used a DIY sanding machine with the coarsest sandpaper and in places got down to the bone.'

'Christ!'

'Charming habits some people have.'

'Is he saying who did it?'

'Claims he fell against a rough brick wall.'

'What's his record?'

'The usual progression from stealing matches from a blind man to robbing helpless old women. Nothing in the big league.'

'Any known connections with drugs?'

'There's nothing on the sheet.'

O'Connor thanked the other and rang off. Newford was a seaside town, declining into seediness, on the north coast, forty miles from Seetonhurst. Assume that this had been a drugs-related assault; that the motive came from a battle over territory. Then it seemed likely that the new mob was spreading its deadly wings very rapidly and very ruthlessly . . .

O'Connor reported to the DI on Wednesday morning. The DI had not had time for breakfast before leaving home and had bought coffee from the vending machine in the canteen.

'I met my informant last night, sir.'

The DI stared down at the paper mug in his right hand as if wondering what was the true origin of what he was drinking.

'The man with a scar on his cheek is meeting someone on Friday night at the Saracen's Head in Stonechurch.'

'And?'

'That's it.'

'Then you must have paid out at something like five quid a word.'

'It tells us where and when.'

The DI drained the mug, crumpled it up and threw it at the waste-paper basket, missed, lit a cigarette. 'D'you know the Saracen's Head?'

'Can't say I do.'

'It's one of the very few pubs that hasn't been tarted up and ruined. But more importantly for the moment, it's a mile outside the village and because the land's as flat as a pancake and there aren't any hedgerows and precious few trees, if you set up a surveillance team nearby, they'll be as conspicuous as honest men in Parliament. You'll have to have someone inside who calls in the team when the time's ripe.'

'I don't like doing it that way.'

'You've no option.'

It was still called a marsh although it had been drained and heavily farmed for many centuries. There were several small villages, a surprising number of churches, some of which had been deconsecrated, and scattered farmhouses.

O'Connor drove through Stonechurch—a dozen old cottages and half a dozen modern houses, a general store, and a wooden community hall—and along the winding lane to the west. The DI had not exaggerated. The land was so open that only distance could hide. Parked cars would be immediately noted and experienced criminals instinctively knew if one was manned by police and not by a couple enjoying private pleasures.

The public house had to the right a single oak, to the left a hedge of privet, but otherwise there was no cover within half a mile. He parked. There were two bars, still called Public and Private. He chose the public bar. Inside were oak beams, a large open fireplace, smoke-stained walls, scarred wooden tables without beer mats, and a smell of beer and—although this had to be an illusion—sawdust.

He ordered a half of Reggie's best (Reginald, the local real ale) and a packet of bacon-flavoured crisps. He chatted with the woman behind the bar who turned out to be far more cheerful than she looked. Searching for something that would be in the police's favour, he decided that in such bucolic surroundings a city villain would stand out like a sore thumb.

CHAPTER 4

'I'll tell you one thing,' said O'Connor, 'you look the part.'

Brent was wearing a T-shirt on which was printed a message that was vaguely obscene if one had a dirty mind, jeans, and trainers; looped over his shoulder was a walkman. 'I even didn't shave this morning and that's zeal beyond the call of duty. Susan reckons that a stubbled chin is the sign of a wop or a cad, or both.'

'Sounds as if she's beginning to see you in your true colours . . . Have you checked transmission?'

'You know me.'

'That's why I'm asking.'

'Transmission's loud and clear.'

'Then get moving. And remember—it could be that you're going to have to spend all evening there, so go very easy on the booze.'

'If you hear me lisping, you'll know I've become immersed in my work.'

O'Connor was briefly annoyed that Brent seemed incapable of ever taking his work sufficiently seriously.

In the evening, a young woman helped behind the bar. A brunette with tightly curled hair, she had generous lips and generous proportions. Brent enjoyed chatting to her so much that he did not notice the newcomer until a man to his right asked, with a note of irritation, for a gin and tonic. The brunette broke off the conversation and moved along the bar to serve the other. Brent turned. The man had a scar on his right cheek. But even though they knew that in appearance their target was no hard-bitten villain, this man looked soft and slack and hardly the type to be involved in the drug scene.

As soon as he'd been served, the man carried the glass over to a corner table and sat. In the mirror, Brent watched him and noted how he repeatedly checked the time. The brunette returned and said what fun it must be to go to France just for the day and he agreed, but did not offer to take her to confirm the fact. After a while, disappointed but not giving up hope, she moved away to have a chat with a regular customer.

Ten minutes later a woman entered the bar, looked around, saw the man with the scar and went over to his table and sat. The man came up to the bar and ordered a whisky and soda, returned. They talked for a time and then he brought out a notebook and pen from his pocket and wrote.

Brent looked at the bar clock. By now O'Connor, wondering what, if anything, was happening, would be as nervous as a grouse on August 12th. Brent left the bar and went through one of the two inside doors to the lavatories; ladies to the right, gentlemen to the left.

There was no one else present. He swivelled the earphones of the Walkman until he could listen on one and speak into the other, pressed down the 'play' switch. 'George to Harry.'

'What the hell's happening?' demanded O'Connor.

'Twenty minutes back a man came in—middle-aged, medium height, overweight, scar on right cheek, soft. Ten minutes ago a woman joined him. She'll never see forty again and if you suggest she was once on the game, I'll not leap to defend her honour.'

'What are they doing?'

'She's talking and he's listening and making notes.'

'Can you get close enough to listen in?'

'No way.'

'Then keep watching and get back to me if anything changes, goods are passed, or they leave.'

Back in the bar, the man with the scar was ordering a second round of drinks and the woman was looking irritated, even angry. The man paid, carried the glasses to the table, and sat. The woman spoke rapidly. He picked up his pen, went to write, then stopped, shook his head. She drank, again spoke at speed. Brent wondered if, contrary to what he'd said to the detective-sergeant, he could get close enough to hear at least a part of what they were saying, but a moment's further consideration brought him back to his original conclusion. Next to them were empty tables and if he settled at one of those he must inevitably draw attention to himself. The woman was streetwise and tough and there was a good chance that if she regarded him closely, she'd identify him as a policeman despite his 'disguise'. There was a saying that was popular in the division. If something's impossible, don't give yourself an ulcer trying to do it, leave that to your superiors. He ordered himself another half pint of Reggie's from the brunette.

They left half an hour later. He waited until the outside door had closed behind them, then went through to the men's lavatory. Once again he was lucky and it was empty. He switched on the transmitter and spoke, at the same time opening the small window sufficiently wide to be able to look out. 'George to Harry.'

'Receiving you.'

'There's been nothing passed between the two of 'em. They're leaving now and returning to their cars. She's making for a blue Jaguar and he's heading for some kind of green Jap car—can't tell the make because with slitty headlamps they all look the same . . . Jaguar is backing and I can now see the number.' He read it off. 'Leaving car park and turning right in westerly direction. The man's having trouble getting the sun to rise—must be one of their Saturday night cars. Or don't they even have Sundays off? . . . He's finally persuaded it to fire on all chopsticks and here's the number.' He read that out. 'He's turning left. Are you going to stop 'em?'

'Can you suggest on what grounds?' replied O'Connor bitterly.

The Detective-Inspector walked from his desk to the window and stared out, hands clasped behind his back. 'It doesn't seem you got much for the money.'

'It's surely too early to say one way or the other,' replied O'Connor. Beforehand, the move had seemed potentially very hopeful; even now, there was still the off-chance that it might prove to be so. The gamble, then, was surely worth many times the two hundred pounds it had cost. But he knew better than really to suppose the problem was that simple. While the public might constantly and justifiably demand better protection from criminals and crime, to provide this would be a very costly exercise. The politicians controlled the purse strings and few wished to be seen to be responsible for increased taxation, so vague promises were made by them, even while they knew that few would ever be implemented because of a shortage of necessary funds. The police in the field had to make do with the tools they were given, no matter how far in quantity or quality these fell short of what they would have liked, and so every penny that was available had to be made to give the best possible value in visible returns. To date, the two hundred pounds paid to Wallace had produced nothing of concrete value; had it been divided among other informers, the chances were that one or more listed crimes would by now have been solved, making for a better clear-up rate and a more contented public . . .

The telephone rang. The DI returned to the desk, spoke briefly, held out the receiver. 'It's for you.'

O'Connor listened.

'Vehicle Registrations here. I've the details of the two car numbers you asked us to check out.'

'Hang on, will you, while I find something to write on?' He brought out his notebook from his pocket and picked up a ballpoint from the desk.

The DI sat, opened the top folder on the desk and began to read the papers inside. He often found it difficult to delegate authority and consequently loaded himself with a mass of work which could and should have been carried out by others.

The short call finished and O'Connor replaced the receiver. He waited until the DI looked up, then said: 'The Toyota is registered in the name of Ashley Hawsley, from Marsham, the Jaguar in the name of Anthony Markland, Hanging Cross . . . Remembering Brent's description of the woman, I'd say it could be well worth asking Records if anything's known about either of them.'

The DI nodded.

O'Connor dialled the number and asked for an immediate identification, as opposed to a detailed one which could take days to reach him.

'Let me know the result,' said the DI, as O'Connor replaced the receiver.

O'Connor returned to his room. The Detective-Inspector's manner had been curt, but he did not suppose that this had been intended as an implied criticism. The relationship between them was purely a professional one and there was seldom reason for unnecessary words; on the few occasions on which they met socially—at the divisional Xmas party, for instance—they had to work hard to keep a conversation going.

Records phoned two and a half hours later. Hawsley was clean. Markland had an extensive record and his last conviction had been for dealing in drugs.

O'Connor went through to the next room, but the DI was

out. He wrote a note and left that on top of the pile of files which had been set exactly in the centre of the desk.

Markland lived in a large house, built in the early 'thirties but Georgian in style, on the outskirts of Hanging Cross. Contrary to popular belief, the village was not so named because a gallows had once stood there, but because *hanen* had been the local word for a triangular-shaped field.

A woman opened the front door. In her early twenties, expensively dressed and made up, the detectives assumed she was Markland's daughter until she made it clear that she was his wife. O'Connor, ever the moralist, wondered what pressures had brought her to marry a man twice her age. Brent, seldom the moralist, wondered whether she made as good a lay as appearances suggested.

She showed them into a large room, facing south, that was furnished in a style which owed everything to money and nothing to taste. She said her husband would be down immediately. Immediately turned out to be eleven minutes.

Markland was a large man whose stomach was beginning to betray both age and gluttony. He had a heavily-featured, pear-shaped face, whose normal expression was sullen aggressiveness. Never a man for subtlety, his opening words were: 'So what d'you bleeding well want?'

O'Connor nodded, informing Brent that he was to start the questioning. They made a good team because O'Connor recognized the strengths and weaknesses of each of them. He was the better interrogator when a quiet, friendly manner was called for, Brent when a touch of roughness was more likely to produce results.

Brent met antagonism with antagonism. 'We're not here to swap compliments, that's for sure. Who was driving your car last night?'

Markland crossed the thick pile carpet to stand in front of the fireplace with its carved marble surrounds. 'So which car are you talking about?' His sneer said that coppers were unused to mixing with people who owned two cars.

'The blue Jaguar.'

'Who says anyone was out in it?'

'If no one was, then it's the first Jag I've ever seen that could get itself down to the Saracen's Head on the marsh.'

Markland was disconcerted, but not panicked. 'Something happen down there, then?'

'Suppose you tell us.'

'How would I know?'

'Provided it was explained to you in words of one syllable.'

'I don't know nothing.'

'Then you weren't even aware that your car was out? You're telling us it was nicked? If it's back now, we'd better take it off to have it checked out.'

'You're not bleeding taking it anywhere.'

'Then maybe you'll start remembering things?'

'Like what?'

'Like who was driving it last night?'

'A friend.'

'What's her name?'

'I didn't say anything about a woman.'

'I'm saying.'

O'Connor took over the questioning. He said, in a quiet, patient voice: 'I imagine the lady who was in the car is a friend of yours?' He didn't lace the word 'lady' with irony.

'Suppose she is?'

'Then we'd like to know her name and where she lives.'

'Why?'

'So that we can have a word with her.'

'What's the shout?'

'We're not accusing her of anything.'

'Was the car in an accident?'

'No.'

'Then you can piss off.'

They left, judging that there was nothing to be gained by continuing the questioning.

On the face of things, the visit had been a fruitless one. Yet they had perhaps, by inference, learned something important. Leaving aside the case of someone who was unwittingly caught up in a crime in which he was likely to be needed as a witness, people were seldom questioned by the police unless they were regarded as possible suspects in identifiable crimes. Therefore if someone who was questioned was innocent of such crime, it was normal for him to do all he could to prove this and cooperation, or the appearance of cooperation, with the police was the first and most elementary course for him to take. Markland had gone out of his way to refuse, and to be seen to be refusing, any cooperation. Then it was likely that he knew that the woman in the Jaguar had been engaged in a criminal activity . . . He had one conviction for drug-dealing. Hawsley had been fingered by an informer as having a connection with drugs . . .

CHAPTER 5

They drove up to the T-junction which marked the centre of the village, waited for an oncoming car, turned right; they passed a general store, a caravan centre, a butcher's, and two small housing estates, one on either side of the road. Over the past thirty years, Marsham had more than doubled in size, but the high cost of housing had ensured that almost all the newcomers were former townspeople who commuted to Seetonhurst or London for work and most of their shopping and who brought with them the blight of suburbanism.

O'Connor, a careful and considerate driver, slowed to a

stop as they approached a fork in the road that was not
signposted. 'Which way now?'

'Take your pick,' replied Brent. 'If you get it wrong the
first time, you're bound to be right the second.'

The narrow lane became a switchback, diving gently
down into dips with grassy banks in which occasional trees
grew, cresting to offer views across the surrounding countryside which, in parts, extended to the marsh.

They found the house as O'Connor finished swearing
because he'd chosen the wrong fork. They turned on to the
gravel drive and parked in front of an outbuilding which
was the garage. One of the sets of doors was open and they
could see inside a green BMW and a deeper shaded green
Toyota.

'How the other half exists!' said Brent. 'They say those
small BMW's are really hot stuff. Wouldn't mind getting
my hands on one.'

They left the car and walked past the second outbuilding
to the narrow gateway in a thorn hedge which gave access
to a well-maintained garden. The house was typical of that
part of the country and had a very long, steeply pitched roof
to the south which left the upstairs floor ten feet narrower
than the ground floor.

O'Connor rang the bell set in the brickwork to the right
of the wooden door, then turned. Beyond the garden the
land sloped away; the marsh was visible and on a really
clear day he judged that probably the sea was as well.
A period house in such a setting had always been his
unattainable ambition; unattainable because he was not
sufficient of a romantic to imagine that he would ever have
enough money to buy one.

The door was opened by a tall, thin woman of indetermi-
nate middle age. Her hair was styled neatly, but without
any touch of imagination, thus matching her frock; her face
was long and made to appear longer by high cheekbones;
one light blue eye was slightly out of kilter and it was

difficult to be certain which; her mouth was straight and
her lips thin and they added to a suggestion of coldness.
She spoke incisively, her voice a trifle high-pitched. 'Yes?'

'Mrs Hawsley? I'm Detective-Sergeant O'Connor and
this is Detective-Constable Brent. I'm sorry to bother you
on a Sunday morning, when you're probably busy with the
roast.' If he had hoped to create a friendly atmosphere, it
became clear that he'd failed.

'What do you want?'

'We'd like a word with your husband, if he's at home?'

She hesitated, then said in tones of sharp annoyance: 'I
suppose you'd better come in.'

Because of the long, sloping roof, the hall was roughly
triangular in shape. To their right were stairs and beyond
these were the kitchen and dining-room; to their left was a
very short passage, off which were three doors.

She ducked under the lintel of the sitting-room door, but
did not bother to warn them to do the same. The room was
square and had a beamed ceiling and one beamed wall.
There was a large inglenook fireplace, in which was a
polished copper hood set above a fire basket and a fireguard
which bore the date 1636.

'I always think that coming into a house like this is rather
like time-travelling,' O'Connor said enthusiastically.

'Really.' She was uninterested in his fanciful comparisons.
'I'll see if my husband can spare you a moment.' She left.

They sat. The room was intimidatingly clean and tidy; the
kind of room in which one was worried by the thought of
knocking something over or of suddenly finding that there
had been something smelly on one's shoes.

Being an old house, there were only floorboards between
the upstairs and downstairs rooms and, despite the carpet-
ing, they could hear a murmur of voices, not clearly enough
to distinguish words, but clearly enough to judge the tenor
of what was being said. She was telling him what to do and
he didn't want to do it.

After a couple of minutes, the murmur of voices ceased. Odd floorboards creaked as weight came on them; then there were the sounds of people descending the stairs. As Hawsley, followed by his wife, entered the sitting-room, the two detectives stood.

Hawsley said: 'You want a word with me about something?'

'That's right,' answered O'Connor. People, with no reason to do so, often became nervous when facing the police; Hawsley, he thought, was more than nervous, he was scared.

'I don't understand . . .'

His wife interrupted him. 'Precisely what is the problem?' She went over to the settee. After a moment's hesitation her husband joined her.

O'Connor sat. 'We've a problem and hope that Mr Hawsley will be able to help us solve it.'

'Most unlikely. He is hardly in the habit of becoming involved in criminal matters.'

'Sometimes that can happen to the most honest of us, Mrs Hawsley. For instance, a person can unavoidably become witness to a vehicle accident where one of the drivers is intoxicated.'

'Are you saying that my husband has witnessed such an accident?'

'No. That was merely an example . . .'

'Then perhaps we could move on and not waste more time?'

'Very well.' His tone remained quietly friendly, but in no way subservient. 'We would like to learn the identity of the lady who was at the Saracen's Head, in Stonechurch, yesterday evening.'

'Then what is the point of your coming here?'

'Your husband should be able to tell us her name.'

'Why?'

O'Connor said to Hawsley: 'You were at the Saracen's

Head last night. What is the name of the lady you met there?'

'I don't know what you're talking about,' Hawsley replied loudly.

'Who is this woman?' asked Mrs Hawsley.

'That's what we're trying to establish.'

'Obviously, I didn't express myself sufficiently clearly. Why do you wish to know her name? Is she a criminal?'

'We can't be certain.'

'Do you really imagine that my husband is in the habit of consorting with people who might be criminals?'

'Surely such a thing is possible if he'd no reason to suspect her?'

She was annoyed, seeing this as an insolent answer which was too well camouflaged for her to be offended by it.

O'Connor said: 'Mr Hawsley, what can you tell us about the lady you met last night?'

'I didn't meet anyone.'

'You're denying that you were in the Saracen's Head last night?'

'It's a ridiculous suggestion.'

'Not so,' said Brent. 'I was sitting at a stool at the bar when you ordered drinks. It's odd you don't remember me, but then maybe your mind was on other things?'

It was possible to judge from the look of panic on Hawsley's face the moment at which his recognitory memory suddenly functioned.

'You arrived at seven fifty-eight. You ordered and drank a gin and tonic at a corner table. At eight eight, a woman joined you and you bought her a whisky. Later, you had a second round of drinks. The two of you left together; she drove off in a blue Jaguar, you in your green Toyota.'

'No.'

Mrs Hawsley said: 'You are completely mistaken.'

'I took the cars' numbers—'

'Kindly don't argue.'

'I wrote the numbers down in my notebook.'

'Then you wrote them incorrectly.'

'I can identify your husband as the man I saw at the bar.'

'You cannot. He was here, in this house, all evening. If you continue to insist otherwise, it's clear that either you're totally incompetent or you have some ulterior motive for lying.'

'The barmaid will identify him; other customers will do the same. You can't really think you'll get away with—'

O'Connor interrupted him. 'If there's no criminal reason to deny the truth, Mrs Hawsley, it'll save everyone including yourselves a great deal of trouble if your husband doesn't. And if it would be embarrassing to both of you to have the details of this meeting made public and we can be certain that there was no criminal element involved, I can assure you that we will do our best to make certain that they remain unpublished.'

She said icily: 'Your inference is quite disgusting.'

O'Connor hesitated, his brow furrowed, then he stood. 'I'm sorry you won't help us.'

They left and their last sight of Hawsley was of a very frightened man. As they walked through the gateway and on to the drive, Brent swore and when they reached the car, he rested his arms on the roof and stared at O'Connor. 'Why the hell did you let that bitch have such an easy ride?'

'What was the alternative?'

'To prove they were both lying as hard as they could go.'

'How?'

'I saw him in the pub, didn't I?'

'She claims her husband was at home all evening.'

'If my evidence isn't enough, there's the barmaid . . .'

'As Mrs Hawsley would no doubt remind you, eye-witnesses' evidence is notoriously inaccurate. Just calm down and look at things as they are, not as you'd have them. In practical terms, we're on thin ice. Their background brands them as naturally honourable and she'd stare any

jury straight in the eye. You need very solid evidence—
which we haven't yet got—before you challenge people like
them too directly.'

'What you're really saying is, because she talks South
Kensington, we need to kowtow.'

O'Connor smiled. 'Sometimes, Jim, you yabber a right
load of bull. If you don't know me better than that, your
IQ must feel weak.' He climbed into the car, waited for
Brent to join him, started the engine, backed.

As they turned into the lane Brent said: 'She'd freeze
alcohol.' He always found it difficult to apologize and this
was his oblique—very oblique—way of doing so.

'Yeah. And for my money, she's frozen at least one part
of his life.'

'Did you note her expression when you were suggesting
he might have been in the pub because he was chasing
nooky?'

'That's one of the possibilities we have to keep in mind.'

'Not after your grass fingered him.'

'He could have got things wrong.'

'Hell! Who's going to chase after a tart that raddled?'

'Some men prefer 'em well worn; it increases their sense
of self-degradation.'

'Move over, Sigmund Freud.'

CHAPTER 6

'It's Sunday and a day of rest,' complained Brent.

'So take an extra five minutes over your lunch,' replied
O'Connor as he drove into the divisional station's car park.
'And when you've done that, see what you can turn up in
the photo albums.' He saw a space at the far end and
steered towards it. 'If there's no joy there, get Reg to
draw up a computer picture and send the result to all

divisions, asking for an ABL.' He parked, switched off the engine. 'Rush Records for the full file on Markland and as soon as that arrives, go through it with a fine-tooth comb for any reference which might possibly help lead us to her. Use your contacts to find out who's working for Markland these days . . .'

'It'd be a whole lot easier to put the screws on Hawsley, since he must realize what a hopeless position he's in.'

'And you think that wife would stand around and let us?'

'She'll try to make it difficult, sure . . .'

'This isn't a case for a bull-headed approach. There's something about it that worries me and until I know more, it's going to be softly, softly . . . Hawsley's about as tough as a sheet of sodden blotting-paper, so how come he's mixed up in the drug trade—when the usual qualification is to be able to slit a man's throat while he's blinking?'

They climbed out of the car. Brent called across: 'What do we know about him?'

'About Hawsley? Nothing. Which is why you're going to start finding out.'

'In my spare time?'

O'Connor grinned as he led the way into the building. They took the lift to the fifth floor and then separated to go to their rooms. He settled behind his desk and began to read through the papers which had come in during his absence and included among these were the weekly and monthly crime statistics. The number of drug-related incidents was continuing to rise with ominous rapidity. He thought of the victims—no less victims because their suffering was caused by their own stupidity and weakness—and knew a renewed hatred for the men and women who had steered them to their fate.

Brent parked in front of the open garage in which was Susan's Porsche. He climbed out of the Escort, locked it, then closed the garage doors and locked them. It didn't

matter how many times he told her that however safe the
neighbourhood might appear there was always someone
around who was ready to nick a very saleable car, she still
left the garage open, and even, on occasions, the ignition
key in the dashboard. It was extraordinary how careless of
their prized possessions the rich could be.

She came out of the sitting-room barefoot, the tails of a
man's shirt hanging over her jeans. She was in a cycle of
casual dress. But give it a few days and she would greet him
in her newest little Cardin number—or whatever was the
latest high fashion. 'I'm sorry I'm so late,' he said, 'but the
work load's doubled.'

'And you have to prove what a great man you are by
volunteering to do the extra?'

'There are no volunteers, only conscripts.'

'And is everyone else as eagerly subservient as you?'

It was going to be one hell of an evening unless he could
find some way of jerking her out of her bad temper. But first
he needed moral support. He went through to the larder
and poured himself out a strong gin and tonic.

She had returned to the sitting-room and was stretched
out on the settee, around which were strewn several maga-
zines. On the nearby occasional table was a three-parts-
empty glass and an ashtray in which were several stubs and
a smoking cigarette. The television was on, but clearly she
had not been bothering to watch it because the pictures
were showing the appalling conditions in which the poor
of Brazil lived and she had no interest in the fate of the
poor.

'Have you had supper?' he asked.

'How could I have? You always demand a hot meal, so
I've just had to wait.'

'There's no need to cook tonight; bread and cheese would
be fine.' He raised his glass. 'Cheers.'

'For God's sake! Can't you ever remember that it's only
the proles who say that?'

'I am a prole. I eat with my mouth open and scoop up peas with my knife—with difficulty. I get drunk every Saturday night and beat up my woman . . .'

'What do female proles do every Saturday night when they're beaten?'

'Shriek.'

'With pleasure, pain, or the pleasure of the pain?'

'What a perverted world you live in.'

'That's why it's such fun. Except on a Sunday night when I'm left on my own and there's no one to get perverted with.' She picked up her glass, drained it, held it out. 'Laphroaig with a third water.'

'You'll find the bottle wherever you left it. Water's in the tap.'

'What a verray parfit gentil knight!'

'What a maiden!'

She laughed and looked younger, warmer and, if that were possible, more desirable. 'What the hell would you do with a maiden?'

'What would you do with a parfit knight?'

'Corrupt him . . . You're no parfit knight, but come and be corrupted.'

'I thought you wanted another drink?'

'Since you didn't have the manners to get me one, I have to make do with second best.'

He finished his drink. 'Your priorities are different from mine and I'm still thirsty.' He crossed to the low table and picked up her glass, left, wondering what the expression on her face signified—fresh anger or amusement?

He poured her out a very large whisky. Drink mellowed her moods, never exacerbated them. And mellowed, she offered him all he had ever hoped to find in a woman . . . If only she had not been brought up in a milieu so wealthy that all her wishes could be satisfied, perhaps, ironically, she would have been satisfied for more of the time . . .

*

Monday morning brought a change in weather. The wind had veered and strengthened, there was a lot of cloud, and the temperature had dropped several degrees.

Inside and to the right of the general store in Marsham was a sub-post-office. Ten years previously a screen of toughened glass had been fitted across the counter and a panic button installed, but otherwise nothing had changed for almost as long as anyone could remember. Miss Hill sat behind the counter, dressed in the conventional good taste of the 'forties, her make-up inappropriate, her toupee obvious, and with unfailing courtesy dispensed stamps, forms, information that was from time to time incorrect, and gossip.

She rubbed the tip of the small wart on the side of her nose. 'I don't think Mr Hawsley from Cockscomb Farm was ever in the army.'

Brent said he was sorry to hear that because then this Mr Hawsley was not the one he sought.

'I'm sure there's no one else of that name who lives around here . . . Of course, there's Mr Heron and he was in the army in the war, but he's been drawing a pension for a long time now. Injured his leg very badly, but they did a wonderful job in the hospital and he hardly limps. His wife's never very well and the doctor's not certain what's wrong with her . . .'

After a while, Brent brought the subject back to the Hawsley who lived locally, but had not been in the army.

'He works for a firm in Seetonhurst which imports wines and spirits—someone said that they're all from Spain, but I wouldn't know about that. He used to be with someone in London, so I've heard, before they moved here.'

Brent wondered what sort of family they had.

'There aren't any children; leastwise, I've never heard of any. Which isn't surprising, really, since she's not what I call a family sort of a person, if you know what I mean.'

Brent said, with too much emphasis—since he was supposed never to have met Mrs Hawsley—that he knew exactly what she meant.

'When I was young, I used to live on the other side of the county and up at the big house there was someone just like Mrs Hawsley. Very good at organizing. She was the chairman of the WVS and something high up in the Red Cross. And since the estate had the living, she always kept a close eye on the parson and made certain he was doing everything she wanted. It was a different world then. I can remember . . .'

He listened to her memories for a while, then thanked her and said goodbye. Back in the car, he sat behind the wheel but did not immediately start the engine. Miss Hill's description of Mrs Hawsley had confirmed the picture in his own mind; a formidable woman of considerable authority. Surely she would have made certain that her husband did not pursue an old scrubber for the obvious reasons? Which confirmed the theory that Hawsley's relations with the woman in the pub had not been of a sexual nature. Yet the reasoning for coming to such a conclusion could not be confined to that incident, but had to be applied to any other that was relevant. In other words, would she ever have allowed her husband to become involved in the drug trade? One could answer that by saying she didn't know what he was doing. But the premise was that she was the kind of woman who would always know what her husband was doing . . . The detective-sergeant had said that there was something screwy about the case. It seemed to Brent that that something might well be Mrs Hawsley's character.

It was to her mother that Caroline Hawsley owed her disturbing ability to be able to know something and yet not to recognize that she knew it.

Unwilling to face the realities of the real world in which longings so often went unfulfilled and disaster was a concomitant of being alive, Caroline's mother had frequently retreated into a world of fantasy. A de Ralais had fought with William the Bastard, but until she had decided that it was so, no one had suggested that Derales was a corruption of de Ralais. The Derales had, in fact, been reasonably prosperous in early Victorian times, but they had never approached the position she claimed for them of being large landowners, with a five-thousand-acre estate in Derbyshire. She had not been proposed to by Lord Uttoxeter, who pledged his love, his wealth, and his life, only to lose the last in the war so that she lost the first and the second. At the age of twenty-five she had married a hard-working engineer who was far too down-to-earth to offer her the knightly romance—though, to her disgust, he did want nightly love—which she believed must be at the heart of any marriage. Her disappointment and disgust had turned her deeper into fantasy. Bewildered, unable to understand her, he had turned to an Irish widow who had seen enough of life to fantasize about nothing. For years after he'd left her, his wife had maintained that he had gone exploring in South America, searching for a lost city whose golden wealth would lift her beyond even her dreams.

Caroline, so often drawn into her mother's strange world, was well into her teens before she could always distinguish between it and the real world; but by then she had learned to enjoy the insidious delight of escaping from reality when that became unwelcome.

No one would ever have called her a beauty. Her features were too sharp, her face too long, her mouth too small; the kind of face often seen on the hunting field. Men were not attracted to her, but in any case she found it difficult to get on with them because Fiona had taught her that love should be the mystical union of two souls, not the physical meeting of two bodies.

Unlike Fiona, there were occasionally times when she wanted to escape, but couldn't. At the age of 33, after the marriage of the last of her closer friends, she had returned home, sat down in front of the dressing-table, and looked in the mirror. She had seen not a maiden awaiting a call to the court of love, but an ageing spinster whose shelf life had already become dangerously prolonged. She had accepted that if ever she was to be married, she must cease to wait for a prince and be content with a man.

Throughout his working life, Hawsley's father had been a clerk with the same firm; for twenty years his mother had worked part-time for a local estate agent. They had been quiet, honest, unambitious people, never having quite enough money because of the demands of the family, but never so hard up that their children went without wholesome food, warm clothes, and those possessions which children had to have if they were to keep their heads held high among their peers.

His brothers and sister had been equally unambitious, seeking only the same kind of life because it had so obviously brought their parents contentment. But he had been different. He was determined to make his mark in the world.

Naturally intelligent, he had worked hard at school and gained a place at a redbrick university; he had come down with a good degree. At that time it had been generally accepted that accountancy offered the best route to commercial fame and fortune and so he had become an accountant. He proved to be a smart one. He could read a page of figures upside down or inside out and if there was even a hint of a loophole in a financial statute, he would identify it. Had he possessed as strong a sense of honesty as his father, he would have risen very high, but his standards were wholly practical. If it paid to be honest, be honest; if it paid to be dishonest, be dishonest. The aim in life was to be rich, not Mr Cleanhands. He had only been with Asteys for a few weeks when he identified a way of enriching himself at no risk . . .

When one was successful it became necessary to show the world that this was so. He rented a flat in Carburrey Terrace, ran a customized Jaguar, and bought his suits in Savile Row; he ate at the most expensive restaurants and tipped the head waiters sufficiently well to overcome their dislike of the *nouveaux riches* to be given good tables; he attended charity balls where he was seen to give generously; he knew a number of influential people who sometimes knew him; he never visited his mother (his father had died), his two brothers, or his sister.

He lived with a succession of women, many of whom would have been reasonably happy to marry him, none of whom could have given him what he still lacked— background. Then he met Caroline Derales. She came from a family which could trace its roots back to the Norman Conquest, had been great landowners in Victorian times, and clearly had breeding. True, she was no beauty, but beauty could always be found elsewhere.

Their marriage could never have been called particularly happy, but since each had had good reasons for welcoming it, they found it offered them compensations . . . Especially Caroline, who was now able to slip into fantasy whenever this suited her. Which she did when he was sacked from Asteys—but not prosecuted since that would have made them look foolish—because his scheme had not been as discovery-proof as he had believed.

He'd thought he understood her reasonably well, but her reactions to his sacking taught him that there were parts of her mind which were, and would probably always remain, a mystery. He had expected her to be shocked, horrified by the proof of his dishonesty, and frightened sick by the prospect of a future without security. In fact, she had merely expressed surprise, seemed not to be interested in why he was sacked, and had expressed a calm confidence that very soon he would get another and better job. A better job than financial adviser to one of the most successful companies in the City?

Incredibly, he had found another and better job; although it had, more accurately, found him. He had been ap- proached by a director of the Seetonhurst Wine Company who told him that the firm was expanding quickly and needed a financial director. He had attended the interview determined to do everything possible to hide the true cause for his leaving Asteys, only to discover later that the reason for his having been sought out was precisely that. He had been offered a salary equal to his previous one and had found it difficult to conceal his grateful surprise that a small country firm should pay so well. His work at first had been perfectly straightforward. Then, after he'd settled in and everything was running smoothly, he'd been asked to arrange a transfer of money which had not gone through the books—as an inducement, he'd been offered a bonus. Since it was the directors who'd asked him and the bonus was considerable, he'd had no hesitation in carrying out the work. There were more unusual commissions and ever-increasing bonuses. Only a fool would have failed to realize that the firm had to be handling something other than wine and spirits.

It was importing hard drugs from Spain. Although he saw nothing inherently wrong in a criminal activity, so long as it went undiscovered, he had always looked askance at the drug trade and had he been called upon actually to handle the drugs or arrange for their distribution, he might have suffered such qualms and fear that, despite the money involved, he would have refused to continue with his work. But all he was ever called upon to do was to check, double check, and treble check, all the figures to make certain no one was swindling the bosses and to arrange the laundering of the money. The kind of work, he was able to reassure himself, that any accountant was called upon to do. A satisfactory conclusion since it meant that he could continue to maintain his standard of living. And later, thanks to another clever move, to raise this by renting a flat and installing Maggie in it . . .

Brent stared at the face on the VDU and after a moment

said that the eyes needed to be slightly more oval in shape. The PC tapped on the keyboard, the face twitched in descending waves, and the eyes became slightly more oval. But they were still not quite right. 'Can you make them smaller?'

'I can turn her into a princess with a tiara, if that's what you want,' said the PC with weary cheerfulness.

'She'd look real odd in a pub on the marsh on a Friday night.'

'Any odder than a bird with half her hair green and the other half blue?'

'You've a point.'

The PC tapped out more instructions and the eyes became smaller. 'How about having another look at the nose? That's always crucial.'

Brent studied the nose. 'That's OK, but there's something wrong somewhere and I can't place what . . .' He'd been trained to remember faces and yet, like most, he found this one of the most difficult tasks to carry out. 'I reckon it's not hard enough looking.'

'Are you serious? Right now, she looks as if she's been on the game since she was five.'

'Try adding a regular beating-up by her ponce.'

The PC scratched his right ear and whistled soundlessly, then tapped out more commands. The face changed. 'Shit! I've got that wrong. She looks like Dracula's widow now. I'll go back . . .'

'Leave it. That's her.'

The PC was momentarily annoyed to have achieved success by a mistake.

O'Connor stared resentfully at the telephone. It had seemingly been ringing all day, yet the one call he wanted had not come through. Fred Wallace had dropped into a very deep hole.

Normally, he could accept that there would in almost

every case be times when no progress would be made. But in this one, each day in which no progress was made meant more victims . . .

Only that morning Pam had told him that he had to stop becoming so emotionally involved. He was doing his best, and therefore to worry himself sick because he couldn't gain results was ridiculous . . . But, thank God, she didn't understand the full extent of the dangers. She still believed that because they had brought up their children to respect decent values, Liz and Harry were safe. But they couldn't be shielded from the youthful urge to buck a danger for the pleasure of proving oneself brave enough to do so, of cocking a snook at what the old people said, of succumbing to peer pressures . . .

Goddamnit, why didn't Fred Wallace ring in?

CHAPTER 7

Brent drove into the car park, his temper worse than when he'd left it a couple of hours before. With six cases in hand and reports on them wanted yesterday, he had had to be landed with obtaining a witness statement, at the request of a North Country force, from a witness who seemed to be understudying the invisible man. Two hours wasted.

One of the civilian typists joined him in the lift. On the journey up, she recounted a piece of risqué gossip, making certain as she did so that her dress was tight across her bosom. Before he met Susan, they'd almost had something going; now, he was vaguely astonished he could ever have found her sufficiently attractive. Let a man learn to enjoy champagne and he lost his taste for lager.

There was one other DC in the general room, typing with unusual fluency. 'I took a message for you, Jim. It's on your desk.'

'Thanks.' He walked over.

'Say, when are you down for your holiday?'

'The first two weeks in August.'

'You wouldn't like to swap for the last two weeks, would you?'

'Sorry. I'm already booked.'

'And you're my last hope . . . So where are you going?'

'Vanua Levi.'

'Where the hell's that?'

'In the Pacific.' He sat, picked up the sheet of paper which lay on top of a file.

'Have you just won the pools?'

'Taken out a second mortgage.' When the question of where they should go for a summer holiday had come up, he had suggested a hotel in Tossa de Mar because he'd been told it was first class by someone who'd stayed there. Susan had laughed because she'd thought he'd been joking. Her hairdresser went to the Costa Brava; everybody's hair-dresser went to the Costa Brava . . .

He read the note. A tentative identification of the com-puter picture had been made by a DC in A Division. It was a woman named Maureen Lewis. He rang Records and asked them to send by wire a copy of her photograph.

The photograph came through twenty-one minutes later. Not crystal clear, nevertheless he was certain that this was the woman whom he'd seen in the Saracen's Head. He tele-phoned Records again and asked for a verbal résumé of her record. Convictions for minor crimes, mostly connected with prostitution; for grievous bodily harm; for drug-trafficking. Her last known address was in Monbridge. He telephoned the Monbridge police and asked them for an L & L on Maureen Lewis, priority. The person to whom he spoke said caustically that in G Division, everything seemed to be priority.

O'Connor returned to the station late Friday afternoon, tired, sweaty, and still feeling resentful. OK, he'd made the wrong decision in the Preston case, but at the time there'd been two possible premises to work to and nothing to suggest which was correct. The DI would have been just as likely to choose the wrong one. But the DI hadn't had to make the snap decision and so he could now, with the benefit of hindsight, sarcastically point out all the mistakes . . .

Brent entered. 'I've been looking for you, Sarge.'

'So now you've found me,' he replied sourly.

Brent recognized the need for discretion. 'D'you remember I made an ID on the woman in the pub? Monbridge have been back on to me. Maureen Lewis quit that address some time ago. One contact said she'd moved south and gave a possible address, but that's proved negative.'

'And?'

'That's where things stand at the moment.'

'Find her.'

'I've sent out an F & D to all divisions and surrounding forces. I've had a word with a couple of contacts and offered them riches beyond their miserable dreams for news of her present whereabouts. I've detailed one of the cadets to talk to as many tarts as he can find to see if one of 'em can prove a lead . . . I reckon that's all I can do for the moment.'

O'Connor had reluctantly to agree. 'Just keep everything moving.'

'Will do.'

Brent left. O'Connor looked at the papers on his desk and then up at the electric clock on the wall. He was going to be late home yet again. Pam was a very understanding wife, but it was Liz's birthday next week and if he missed out on the party, he'd find that Pam's understanding could come to a very sharp stop.

A man who liked to keep in good physical shape and every morning, rain or shine, jogged through North Common was passing one of the several stands of trees in the southern half of the common when he heard a noise which brought him to a stop. A kind of buzzing, but so loud that he couldn't begin to place its possible origin. He looked at his watch; five minutes in hand. He stepped off the path and crossed the grass to the trees which, despite the passage of people, had patches of bramble around them. The buzzing was coming from behind one of these. Instinctively apprehensive without knowing why, he moved forward and round and saw a huge swarm of bluebottles on a bundle of rags. Someone had left some rotting food in among the rags . . . And then, sickeningly, he realized that the bundle of rags had once been a human being.

Wrapped in a body-bag, the dead man was taken in an undertaker's van—corpses were not carried in ambulances—to the mortuary in the suburb of Croxley.

The building dated from the late nineteenth century and from the outside looked like a private house—Croxley had once been a fairly fashionable suburb and therefore it had been deemed necessary to mask the realities. Inside, however, everything was late twentieth century; overhead light pods, tilting tables, stainless steel sinks, sterilizing cabinets, and cold compartments which held mortal corruption at bay.

An assistant pathologist conducted a brief, external-only examination, prior to the corpse's being loaded into one of the cold compartments. After he'd stopped talking into the microphone by the side of the examination table, he turned to the PC who was duty coroner's officer. 'Death by suffocation after an extensive application of violence; or, to put it more succinctly, torture.'

'Torture!' repeated the PC, surprised because he had assumed that the various visible injuries had been inflicted in a struggle.

'Very unsophisticated and owing nothing to modern electrical or chemical techniques. Nails and teeth torn out, that sort of thing. You'll want dabs, of course. I'll take them.'

In the past, a police officer had taken the prints, but it had become recognized that when it came to corpses, the skill of a pathologist was likely to be greater. He took each print in turn, gripping the finger or thumb firmly at the first joint and rolling it first across an inked pad and then across the glossy paper.

The prints were sent, via a patrol car, to county HQ. Here, a computer system for the classification of fingerprints had been under evaluation for a year, resulting in a division of personnel into those who believed it was quicker, easier, and more efficient, and those who maintained it was next-door to useless. On this occasion it worked admirably. Within three minutes it identified Frederic Wallace.

O'Connor stared down at the report. Frederic Wallace, 63, last known address, 24 Cheriton Road, Wickton. A long record of minor crime.

The murder seemed to make one thing clear. Hawsley was for certain tied up with the drugs ring since it must have been the questioning of him which had triggered this barbaric killing—that the police had known of the meeting between him and Maureen Lewis must mean that they had been given the information by an informer. With brutal efficiency, the men running the organization, having pre-viously identified him as a possible suspect, had picked him up and tortured him into confessing, then murdered him. Maureen Lewis had been told either to disappear or had also been murdered, if that were the safer solution, and one day her body might be discovered. That Hawsley had also not disappeared must mean either that he was too valuable to the organization or that he was considered to be not at any real risk. Certainly, with Maureen vanished and Wal-lace dead, there was nothing legally admissible to tie him in with the drugs scene . . .

The more he considered the facts, the more O'Connor

realized that the police had completely lost the initiative. He swore. Every day that passed meant more victims, yet now the police were no nearer to success than they had been on the day Wallace had first spoken of the man with a scar on his cheek. Normally, O'Connor would have viewed Wallace's death with shocked horror, but for the moment he could only be profoundly and bitterly infuriated by it.

Pamela O'Connor sometimes joked that she was lucky since she could be certain Hugh loved her for herself, not for her looks. Twenty years before she could never have said such a thing because then her appearance had caused her endless humiliation. It had taken maturity, marriage, and a family, to teach her her own worth.

She had an overlong face in which each feature seemed to be out of proportion; there was a large, unsightly mole just below her left eye; her nose was, to put it gently, Roman; there was a patch of eczema around her left ear which defied any and every cream that was tried; her hair was mouse-brown and dead straight; only her large, soft brown eyes were beautiful.

She was a very happy woman. In a world where consumerism made for discontent, she asked only for what she already had—a loving husband, two healthy children, a nice home, and just sufficient money. All the time she possessed these, she was untroubled by outside problems. Let there be international sabre-rattling, currency upheavals, or fearsome trade disputes, and she viewed these crises with complete equanimity. But let her family or her home be threatened and the Four Horsemen rode fast and furiously. If Harry was only ten minutes late home, she prepared to phone the local hospital to discover to which one he'd been taken; if Liz fell and scratched herself, she frantically recalled the date of Liz's last tetanus jab . . .

'For once you're back at a reasonable time, love,' she

said as she greeted O'Connor in the small hall of their semi-detached with a light kiss on the cheek.

'I decided I needed an early night.'

'Which you most certainly do! You're looking all baggy around the eyes. Go and watch the telly and I'll start supper. I've bought you a pork chop; you'll like that, won't you?'

'With fried onions?'

She smiled. 'Would I dare forget 'em . . . Hurry on in and start watching; there's a wildlife programme coming on soon and you love them.'

He nodded, even though it wasn't really true any longer. There were so many wildlife programmes that he'd begun to be bored by them unless they were unusual. 'Are the kids all right?'

'Liz is at the Wilsons' and I'm to collect her later on, Harry's upstairs doing his homework.'

'Or hoping that we'll believe he is.'

'Come on, Hugh, that's not being fair. He really has been working quite hard recently. His marks in the last test were much better.'

'Start from right down and they can only get much better.'

'You mustn't be so hard on him.'

'When I was his age—'

'I'll bet you had a copy of Sexton Blake inside your maths book.'

He smiled, because he could remember telling her not so long ago how he'd done just that in a geography lesson and had been caught and subsequently taught the error of his ways.

'Now go and sit down and I'll start the cooking. And have a drink to buck yourself up.'

'If you'll have one as well?'

'Me? I'm fine.'

He poured out a sweet sherry for her and a half pint of canned best bitter for himself, then settled in the front room and half-watched a quiz show, not the wildlife programme, happy to let his mind drift.

They ate half an hour later, seated at the table in the dining-room. When it came to their lifestyle, he was, as in so many things, old-fashioned, holding as firmly as possible to the manners which his parents had taught him; only occasionally, could he be persuaded that they should eat on their laps as they watched a TV programme.

She served him a generous helping of trifle, one of his favourite sweets despite its association with childhood, and then looked at the little that was left in the bowl. 'You can finish it, can't you?'

'I don't know so much.'

'Come on. I thought you really liked it?'

'I do, but it's only last week that you said I was putting on weight.'

'When you come back home all black-eyed, you need feeding up, however stout you're getting. Now, give me your plate—' She stopped as the phone rang. 'I wonder if that's Liz, wanting to be picked up early?'

'One way of finding out would be to answer. I'll go.'

'No, you won't. It might be for you and if it is, and it's the station, I'm going to tell them you're out and I've no idea when you'll be back.' She hurried out of the room.

He began to eat. The trifle was exactly to his liking. More whipped cream than sponge, a strong flavour of alcohol . . .

She returned and he knew immediately that she'd received bad news. 'Is it Liz?' he asked, experiencing the tightening of sudden fear.

She shook her head, sat.

They were on their own because Harry had returned upstairs after the first course. 'What's up, then, love?'

'That was Norma. Paul's in trouble.'

'What kind?'

'He tried to mug an old woman and is in custody.'

'That's ridiculous.'

'He was caught doing it.' She sighed. 'It seems he was on drugs and was trying to steal enough money to buy some. Norma didn't even suspect he was an addict until the police called her and Maurice along to the police station.'

'Oh my God!' he said thickly. All sense of the peace which his homecoming had given him was gone and he was back with the bitter problems which had been frightening him for so long. The Prideaux family were so similar in background and way of life to their own that Paul's arrest for a drug-related incident was the most potent confirmation possible of his fearful certainty that every family was at risk, no matter how united they might be. That risk was closing in on him. He would place his soul at stake to go on oath that Harry had never yet experimented with any drugs, but he would not, could not, do the same for the future. And he experienced a growing sense of guilt that this should be, because although he could be certain that a vicious drugs ring was becoming more and more active, yet he was doing nothing to destroy it simply because the law would not let him act until he had the necessary proof.

CHAPTER 8

O'Connor would have had great difficulty in formulating his moral standards, not simply because he had always found it difficult to analyse his own thoughts, but because he liked to think of himself as a logical man. While right was right and wrong was wrong, he was uneasily aware that however much he might have liked there to be absolutes, there weren't any and at times right became wrong and wrong became right. And because the law could never make such an admission, it was left to the individual who helped to administer it to ensure that justice was done. Yet the doing of it could be nearly impossible because a policeman gained his authority from the law and therefore mustn't be seen to be undermining it . . .

Theory said that it was not the police's job to convict criminals, but to uncover the evidence that would lead to their conviction. The police were neutral and evidence had to be neutrally adduced and presented. But how neutral could a detective be if certain beyond the shadow of a doubt that a man was guilty? How could he neutrally stand by and watch a criminal continue to commit crime which injured innocents simply because he could not uncover the evidence which a court demanded before it would judge? How could he live with the knowledge that those who were injured, in part at least, owed their injuries to him? It was wrong to fake evidence, but it had to be right to do whatever one could to prevent the innocent being injured. If faked evidence convicted a criminal who had committed a crime, was that right or wrong? To say that until a man was convicted by a court of law it was impossible to call him guilty, was to live by the theory of the law, not the practice in the market-place. The age-old struggle between the idealist and the pragmatist; between those who lived in ivory towers and those who lived on the streets.

He could argue with himself for as long as he liked, but he knew what most of his fellow policemen would say: he was a bloody fool even to contemplate the action he had in mind. But then they were being traitors to themselves and to the justice they were meant to serve, since they were hiding behind the rules and the regulations because these would defend them just as they defended the criminals.

He knew the risks involved and what would happen if he were caught. He knew that to most people, his intended action would seem to be totally out of character. Yet when he thought of Liz and Harry, he knew it to be wholly in character.

He took the lift down to the ground floor and then the stairs to the first basement. The property room was unlocked and a uniform PC was, without any enthusiasm, making an inventory of stolen property recovered the previous night.

'I need a quick dekko,' O'Connor said.

'Help yourself,' replied the PC.

'Where's the key to the box?'

'Hanging up behind the door.'

O'Connor crossed to the door and swung it back until he could remove the key from the cup hook on which it had been hanging.

At the far end of the oblong room were four shelves, on three of which were stored small items; on the fourth was the strongbox, made from sheet metal and channelling. He unlocked this. Inside were two piles of plastic sachets, one small, one nearly twice the size; the contents of all of them were slightly off-white in colour and had the apparent texture of flour. Careful to keep his back to the PC, he reached inside, picked up one of the sachets, and palmed it. 'Is this all that's frozen?'

'That's all that's in right now, yeah.'

'I thought we'd had a big bust inside the last twenty-four hours?'

'If so, no one's been down to put the stuff on ice.' The strongbox was known as the fridge, the confiscated drugs which were put inside it were either frozen or on ice.

'Then I've had a wasted journey.'

'No need to panic. You're being paid.'

'That's all you youngsters think about,' said O'Connor, with mock disapproval.

'We've learned to get our priorities right, haven't we?'

'Depends where you're standing . . . Let me know if another load does come in, won't you?' O'Connor was certain the request would be forgotten.

'Sure thing,' replied the PC, already forgetting.

O'Connor left, for once grateful that so many of the younger PCs were slack in a way that would never have been tolerated when he had first joined the Force. Not only should he have signed the log on entering Property, the PC should have made certain that he signed a second log before opening the strongbox. As it was, there was no written record of his visit. The gods were obviously with him.

O'Connor used the internal phone to call Brent to his office. Brent, who'd been struggling to complete a bureaucratically incomprehensible form, arrived looking as bad-tempered as he felt. 'Are you busy?' O'Connor asked.

'Me? Been sitting about wondering how to make the time pass until I can honestly leave for home.'

'Wonder no longer. We're on our way for another chat with Hawsley.'

Brent sat on the edge of the desk. 'Has something fresh come in?'

'No.'

'Are you going to lean on him hard?'

'No.'

'Then where's the point?'

'To see if he's had second thoughts about helping us.'

'You must be the original optimist.'

'It could be different. She's not going to be there to prop up his backbone.'

'How d'you know?'

'She's chairman, or chairwoman, or whatever the hell they say, of the parish council and it's their annual general meeting; starts at six.'

'You don't miss a trick,' said Brent admiringly.

O'Connor checked the time. 'If I'm any judge of character, she'll leave early to start organizing everyone. So if we move now, we should find him in and her out.'

They went down to the ground floor and out through the rear entrance to the car park. One of the three CID cars was in and they took this. Brent drove and began the journey by chatting, but O'Connor seemed to have suddenly become morose and he answered only in monosyllables. Brent, perplexed by this abrupt change, switched his thoughts to a more pressing question—what did he give Susan for her birthday? What could he buy that she wanted but did not already have and he could afford?

They turned into Cockscomb Farm and parked in front of the garage. One set of doors was open and only the Toyota was inside. They walked round to the front of the house. Brent rang the bell and after a brief wait the door was opened by Hawsley, whose immediate fear was unmistakable.

'Have you time for a bit of a chat?' asked Brent.

'What . . . what d'you want?'

'Like I just said, a chat.'

'I'm . . . busy.'

'We won't keep you . . . That is, if you tell us what we need to know.'

Hawsley tried to assert some authority. 'You'll have to come back another time.'

'Between you and me, we're so strapped for time that it's now or never.'

There was no doubt which Hawsley would have preferred.

'What say we go and have a sit-down while we chat?' Brent's breezy, self-confident manner was designed to make Hawsley feel he had to agree.

They went into the sitting-room. The television was switched on, a newspaper was open on the settee, and a half-full glass was on one of the occasional tables, giving the room an air of being lived in, something it had lacked the last time they'd seen it.

Brent sat and started the questioning. 'We've been learning about Maureen.'

The name shocked Hawsley.

'She's quite a lady—always assuming that's the word to use. You obviously like 'em rough and tough.'

'I don't . . . I don't know who you're talking about.'

'Maureen Lewis, the woman who you had a couple of

drinks with at the Saracen's Head nearly a fortnight ago.'

'I told you, I've never been there . . .'

'Yeah, yeah. Can't really blame you for lying when the wife's listening in. Not very broad-minded, is she?'

'You've no right to talk like that.'

Brent thrust his chin out. 'If I was you, I wouldn't try pushing us around. Kind of makes us mean-minded.'

'I swear I don't know any woman by that name.'

'Find a stack of Bibles and swear on 'em for a couple of hours if that's what keeps you amused, but you'll still be a liar. Why did you and Maureen meet up?'

'I didn't . . .'

'We've been showing your photo around. The barmaid and a regular at the Saracen's Head picked you out immediately. I saw you there. So you really want to go on denying it? Because if you do, you know what that means, don't you?'

Hawsley made no answer.

'It means you were up to some villaining.'

'I wasn't.'

'Then why not admit you were there?'

'It . . . it wasn't me.'

'You're telling us you have a twin brother? It was you. And since I'd say you'd have to have been shipwrecked for a dozen years on a desert island before she'd even start to look exciting, it wasn't nooky you were after. The only other thing she has to offer is drugs. You and she were doing a deal, weren't you?'

'No.'

'Come on, admit it. Where's the point in denying something as obvious as a bikini at Ascot?'

'No,' he shouted wildly. Beads of sweat had begun to stand out on his face.

'Hasn't anyone ever explained how you make things much worse for yourself by lying? Explain how things were now and we're sympathetic. Keep on lying and we're annoyed. And when that happens, we're liable to—'

O'Connor interrupted him. 'That's enough of that.'

'All I'm doing—'

'There's no call for getting nasty.'

'No call, when he won't admit the truth? What about—'

'What about you belting up? Go out to the car and bring me the folder that's on the back seat.'

Brent hesitated, then stood. He glared at Hawsley, strode out of the room—escaping disaster only at the last moment when he remembered to duck under the lintel—and slammed the door shut behind himself. He grinned. There was a ham actor in every detective.

He left the house and strolled round to the car, taking his time because O'Connor would now be apologizing for his detective-constable's aggressive crudity. He'd offer sympathetic understanding, gently point out that although nothing could be promised, cooperation earned goodwill, and generally arouse Hawsley's relieved gratitude to the point where it must seem to him that the only reasonable thing to do was to tell the truth.

Brent leaned against the car, lit a cigarette, and stared across the field beyond the garage as he once again tried to decide what to buy Susan for her birthday . . . He heard the approaching car, but beyond automatically judging from the sounds that it was travelling very fast for a country lane, he took no direct notice of it until it turned into the drive. The BMW was braked fiercely to a skidding halt on the gravel. Mrs Hawsley climbed out. 'What are you doing here?' she demanded.

He cursed the bad luck which had brought her back. 'We need to ask your husband a few more questions.'

'Who is we?'

'Detective-Sergeant O'Connor and myself.'

'Where is he?'

'In the house.'

'Neither of you has the slightest right to be here. I shall instruct our solicitors to complain very forcefully about this.'

Each word was frozen, bitten off, and spat out. She turned and walked towards the garden. He followed her, matching stride for stride and having to move energetically to keep up.

When she entered the sitting-room she came to a sudden stop as she stared at her husband who was cringing back against a chair, one hand held in front of his face. He burst into a torrent of febrile speech, virtually incoherent because of fear.

Brent's attention was caught not by either of the Hawsleys, but by O'Connor. He had seen guilt too often not to recognize it.

She overcame her sense of shock and crossed to her husband's side. 'What's been going on?' she demanded.

'He says . . . I didn't . . . He can't have . . .'

'Pull yourself together. Have they been assaulting you?'

He shook his head.

'Then what is the matter?'

The strength of her presence helped him to regain a measure of self-control. He pointed at O'Connor. 'He's trying to say the packet of drugs was in my pocket. But it wasn't. He put it there.'

She swung round to face O'Connor. 'Do I understand that you're trying to claim you've found drugs in my husband's possession?'

O'Connor said: 'There was a sachet in his right-hand pocket which may or may not prove to contain a substance prohibited under the acts. The contents will have to be analysed in a forensic laboratory before we know for certain what they are.'

'He put it in my coat pocket,' Hawsley shouted. 'He said that if I wouldn't tell him the truth about that woman, he'd have me arrested for drug-peddling.'

She faced O'Connor. 'Get out of this house.'

They left.

CHAPTER 9

'Goddamnit!' said O'Connor bitterly, 'he was just about to talk.'

Brent changed down and braked for a sharp corner. 'You must have gone round the bloody twist. What in the hell made you try such a dangerous game?'

'I had to make him talk. I knew he'd break if I put real pressure on him.'

'I suppose you realize that it's more than likely that it's yourself you've broken?'

'He won't dare complain.'

'You can't be that blind. She's just got to be on the blower right now, telling the family solicitors to start shouting.'

'She's not a fool, whatever else she may be; she won't dare risk the publicity.'

'You're supposing she knows what he's been up to?'

'She must.'

'Then she'll probably also know that we can't prove a thing.'

'Yes, we can. His dabs are on the sachet.'

'Big deal . . . Until you're up on a charge of planting evidence and the prosecution shows how you tricked him into handling it.'

'You're missing the point. They can't be certain how little we know and guilty people always fear the worst.'

'You're trying to walk on moonbeams. Whatever she now knows, she's going to teach you a lesson for daring to try to kick her husband around. She's a vindictive bitch and will do everything possible to see you blasted.'

They rounded another corner which brought them to a longish straight and Brent accelerated fiercely since the speed temporarily eased a little of his worry.

O'Connor said: 'You really think she will put in an official complaint?'

'I'll give a thousand to one on it.'

There was a short silence.

'Why did she have to turn up? I had him on the run.'

O'Connor, Brent noted, was now sounding plaintive rather than resentful. He was beginning to realize that the consequences of his actions would probably be catastrophic for himself.

'I had to do it, Jim.'

'Why?'

'Because of Paul Prideaux.'

'Who's he?'

'The son of friends of ours; a decent kid from a decent family, brought up just like my two. He was arrested the other day for trying to mug an elderly woman. He's on the hard stuff and needed the money to buy a fix. The parents didn't suspect a thing until his arrest. Pam saw them and says they're both totally shattered. There are dozens of families like that and if this new mob isn't busted very soon, there'll be thousands.'

'Why couldn't you work things legally?'

'Because we haven't been getting anywhere. Because I've two kids and I can picture what it would be like to discover that one of them is a druggie. You don't have kids, Jim, so you dont understand . . .'

Suppose it had been Susan under threat. He'd kill to protect her. 'I understand,' he said quietly.

They passed the 30 m.p.h. sign, the town sign, and the first of the town houses. They turned right at the corner on which was the large, ugly building which had once been a reformatory school but now housed council offices.

'It'll be one against one,' said O'Connor, breaking a silence that had lasted a couple of minutes.

'D'you remember telling me something? People like them always start off by carrying extra clout just because of their background. All the time we can't prove anything against them, they're carrying that clout.'

'Juries tend to believe policemen.'

'They used to, back in the days when the public loved their bobbies. Now they don't love 'em so they disbelieve 'em when they can. And even should they believe you, will the DI?'

'How's he come into it?'

'You're not thinking straight. Maybe you make lucky and this never reaches the court, but if that bitch lodges a complaint, there'll have to be some sort of internal inquiry . . . The DI is always so careful not to favour his own that he practically demands a copper has St Peter as a witness before he'll believe him.'

'You're a real comfort.'

A realist, Brent thought.

There was another silence which he didn't break until they were within half a mile of divisional HQ. 'This packet you planted on him—what's in it, flour?'

'Happy powder.'

'Coke! Jesus!' The car swerved and he had hastily to steer to the left. The driver of an oncoming car hooted. 'Where in hell did you get that from?'

'Property. I knew there'd been a couple of busts recently and the take was still on ice. I reckoned that if I had the real thing—and Hawsley would recognize it for what it was—I could flash it and that would break him. Only it wasn't really necessary. The moment he touched the sachet, he was so scared he'd have told me the lot if only that bloody woman hadn't turned up.'

'If you went down to Property, you signed. The first thing anyone is going to do when trying to work out who's the liar is to check the log books. When your name's found, it's not going to need a computer to add two and two together.'

'I didn't sign either log book.'

'How come?'

'The youngster on duty was too bored to bother.'

'Then thank your lucky stars for inefficiency and don't ever moan about the modern generation again.'

They had to wait opposite the entrance into the divisional car park for oncoming traffic before Brent was able to pull across the road. He parked alongside his own Escort. 'I've been thinking. It's no good just hoping, so you're going to have to work on the assumption that the Hawsley woman will raise as much hell as she can, provided only that it doesn't expose her husband for the shit he is. In the ensuing inquiry, inevitably there'll be a check to see if you nicked one of the fixes from the strongbox in Property. They won't be content with accepting you didn't just because the books aren't signed by you, they'll get hold of the duty PC and question him. And when he's leant on, the odds have to be that he'll remember your visit and admit to it because he won't want to be suspected of complicity. Let them be certain you opened up the strongbox and you never signed and you can't explain and they'll have you. So you've got to move fast to cover your tracks.'

'How can I? It's no good trying to sign retrospectively, not when the books are ruled off every twenty-four hours.'

'Cut the powder you have and make a second pack the same size as the original. Return one to the pile from which you took it, which is what you were going to do anyway, and name the other as having come from Hawsley's pocket. The best defence is attack.'

Brent opened the car door and stepped out. He hoped he'd managed to help the detective-sergeant avoid the consequences of having too sharp an imagination and too developed a social conscience.

Pam greeted her husband in the hall, then studied his face. 'Is something wrong, love?'

He shook his head.

'Are you certain?'

'Of course I am.'

'But you look so worried.'

He tried to make a joke of it. 'That's just my relaxed expression.'

She ignored his answer. 'Has something happened at work?'

'Haven't I just said, nothing's wrong.'

'Yes, but . . . Maybe you're too tired . . . I've made a hotpot for supper. I hope you don't think it's too warm for that? When Liz saw me doing the cooking, she said she thought it was daft having a hotpot in the middle of the summer.'

'Offer her bread and margarine instead and see if she still finds it silly. Are she and Harry OK?'

'Why d'you ask?'

'Is it such an odd thing to do?'

'But you said it in such a way . . . Well, almost as if you're scared something could have happened to them.'

He spoke far more seriously than he had intended. 'Things can always happen.'

'You're worried about them because of Paul, aren't you? But they'd never do anything like that.'

'You'd have said the same about Paul until the other day.'

She could not deny that.

'We've done all we can,' he said heavily. 'Now all we can do is leave it to them.'

'They know what's right, Hugh.'

'Then they're lucky.' He realized that in saying that he'd made a big mistake. She was once more studying him with worried unease. 'What I mean is, they're lucky they've got you to teach them.' It was a lame explanation, but it seemed to satisfy her. 'Have we any milk powder, love?'

She was surprised by the sudden change in conversation. 'I use it when I make yoghurt; if I don't, quite often it won't set. I've often wondered if they're doing something to the milk in the bottles to try to stop people making their own yoghurt so that they'll have to buy it in the shops.'

'That sounds like a good capitalist idea. Where is it?'

'In a tin in one of the cupboards in the kitchen. Why d'you want it?'

'To take some to the station to see if it'll make the coffee taste less like syrup of figs.'

'Why won't you let me make the coffee and put it in a Thermos for you?'

'Because you've more than enough to do as it is, without me adding to it.' He went through to the kitchen and she followed him, told him which cupboard to look in. To add verisimilitude to the story, he asked her how much powdered milk she thought he should put in a cupful of coffee. He measured four teaspoonfuls into a plastic bag. He said he'd some work to clear up before supper and would she give him a call when the meal was ready.

He went upstairs. From the first bedroom he passed came the harsh beat of pop music—Harry's taste in music was not his—and from the second, the chatter of voices—Liz and one of her friends were exchanging confidences, or whatever it was that twelve-year-old girls exchanged. He entered the third bedroom and crossed to the small table which he used as an occasional desk. He brought from his pocket the plastic bag with the milk powder in it and the much smaller sachet containing the coke. With a razor blade, he slit open one corner of the smaller bag and then tipped the contents on to a sheet of glossy paper. He stared at the tiny heap of off-white powder. Incredible that anything which looked so innocuous could be possessed of such demonic powers.

He used the razor blade to separate the coke into two equal quantities, then to each he added enough milk powder to make it the same size as the original. With the help of the blade and a tube of adhesive, he made a second sachet and then filled both with the—now twice adulterated—

coke. He sealed the open sides, put each sachet into an unused envelope.

He carried the glossy paper through to the lavatory, tore it up into little pieces, and flushed these away. He washed the razor blade with soap and water, slipped it into the dispenser at the back of a pack of five blades, carried the pack down and put it into the dustbin which would be emptied the next morning.

'Have you finished the work?' Pam asked.

'I've done all I can without nipping back to the station for five minutes after supper.'

Her annoyance was immediate. 'For heaven's sake, what you need is to relax, not go back there.'

'Sorry, but I must. I won't be gone more than ten minutes.'

Property was locked. O'Connor went up the stairs to the ground floor and along to the front room. There were no members of the public present and the duty sergeant and PC, behind the counter, were talking to a couple of uniform PCs. 'Who's on Property duty?' O'Connor asked.

The duty PC said reluctantly: 'I suppose I am, Sarge.'

'Then go on to suppose that you open up for me.'

'Don't you ever go off duty?' He searched under the counter for the key, straightened up. 'Are you wanting to use the strongbox?'

'I am.'

'Then you'll need that key as well.'

'Good thinking. You'll do well in your sergeants' exams.'

'He's too bright for that,' said one of the other PCs.

The duty PC led the way down to Property. He unlocked the door and stood to one side so that O'Connor entered first. 'Don't forget to sign on, Sarge.'

'Where's the book, then?'

'To your right.'

O'Connor wrote down his name, rank, time, and signed the entry. 'Where's the book for the strongbox?'

'On the table somewhere. Leastwise, that's where it was.'

It was under several sheets of memoranda. He listed his reason for needing access—to deposit one sachet, contents undetermined, previously in the possession of Mr A. Hawsley. He walked to the far end of the room, unlocked the strongbox, put his right hand into his pocket. 'Is that someone shouting?' The question diverted the PC's attention while he brought both sachets out of his pocket and put one on the larger of the existing two piles and the other to one side, on its own.

'Can't hear anyone,' said the PC.

O'Connor, a crumpled-up envelope in the palm of his hand, shut the door and locked it. 'It must have been my tinnitus.'

'What's he when he's at home?'

'Ringing in the ears. It's something which comes with age.'

The PC was still young enough to view with amusement the afflictions of the aged. 'So who was playing just now—St Clement's?'

CHAPTER 10

Susan emptied the bottle of Nuits St Georges into their two glasses. 'Don't let anyone fool you that you're good company. You've been staring blankly into space for the past ten minutes.'

Brent said: 'I was thinking about Hugh. He has a problem.'

'So what's new? Does he ever have anything else?'

'It's because he suffers from a social conscience.'

'How boring!'

'You should be grateful that there are people who do have such things.'

There was a faint smile on her face. 'Are you often troubled by the do-good syndrome?'

'I hope so . . . You don't like Hugh, do you?'

She put a cigarette in the long jade holder—a newly acquired habit—and lit it. 'I'm sure he's a very worthy man.'

'Which in your eyes damns him beyond redemption?'

'You're very pugnacious tonight. Perhaps it's because you've been eating too much red meat . . . Worthy men make for poor company. The last time we had dinner at Hugh's place, he never stopped talking about the iniquities of the local council's housing policy. Hardly the material of scintillating conversation.'

'Yet vital to anyone who can't find a roof to fit over his head.'

'You know your trouble? At heart, you're a Puritan. You have one of those awkward consciences which tells you it's wrong to enjoy yourself; so if you are, you desperately search for some reason to stop doing so. Tell me something: have you begun to look around for a reason to get rid of me?'

'You're talking nonsense to annoy me.'

'I do like irritating you because it makes you so aggressive and then you're very sexy. But, you know, it is a fact that you become uneasy if you discover you're enjoying life too much . . . Shall I let you into a little secret? If ever I think you're searching for a reason to get rid of me, I'll pull the rug from under your feet by clearing out first.'

'In order to salve your self-esteem.'

'Well, well, well! You're beginning to understand me . . . Let's open another bottle and drink to our clever selves.'

Brent arrived at divisional HQ ten minutes late; a not unusual occurrence. He parked his car, climbed out and locked it, began to walk towards the building.

'Jim.'

He turned, searching for the detective-sergeant.

'I'm over here.'

He saw O'Connor at the wheel of his car and went across. 'Get in.'

He climbed into the front passenger seat.

'D'you know what's happened?'

'How could I when I've only just arrived?'

'Becker and Lampson put in an official complaint first thing this morning.' They were the leading firm of solicitors in Seetonhurst; while much of their work was in the traditional line of country practices, somewhat unusually one of the partners had made a considerable name for himself in criminal law because of his robust, aggressive style.

'Like I said, that had to be expected.'

'Yeah, but I'll bet you didn't expect them to say that Mrs Hawsley was in the house from the time we arrived and she'll swear that I tried to plant a packet on her husband.'

'But . . .' Brent laughed.

'What's so funny?' O'Connor demanded angrily.

'Can't you see? You're lying your head off and so now she's lying her head off.'

'And you think that's bloody hilarious?'

'No, of course not. All I meant—'

'With the two of them against me, I haven't a chance. I'm for the bloody high jump.'

Brent couldn't deny that. 'Has the old man said anything yet?'

'Not to me because I've not been up to my room. I met Sid when I arrived and he told me. Jim, what am I going to do? You know what it means, don't you? With the two of 'em backing each other up, I'll be slaughtered. I'll be convicted and that means I'll be out of the Force.'

Not to mention the inevitable prison sentence, thought Brent. But it became clear that O'Connor's worries were not for himself.

'I'll lose the pension. There'll be nothing to keep the family on. What's it going to be like for them, everyone knowing what's happened? The other kids'll take it out on Liz and Harry. A whole squad of little bastards shouting, "Your father's a crook; your father's a crook." And the neighbours will shun Pam. There's still a long way to go on the mortgage of the house and if I can't keep paying, they'll repossess. Where can Pam and the kids go to live? Her mother's place is far too small and my father's in a home. Christ, Jim, what can I do?'

It was not the first time Brent had been asked the question. Many men were totally bewildered to discover that they would have to face the consequences of their crimes. But this was the first time that he had been asked the question by a man who had had no intention of benefiting from the crime he had committed. The O'Connors were a family he had often envied because they had always seemed so complete. Susan mocked them for being so ordinary; he saw this as one of their strengths.

'I . . . I don't know what to do.' O'Connor sounded choked.

There was much of a gambler in Brent; not the steely-eyed man who assessed the odds and only played when these favoured him, but the quixotic one who assessed them emotionally and so often played with foolhardy recklessness. 'It's a liars' convention, so why don't I join in?'

'I don't know what you mean.'

'It started off as one against one; she's made it two against one; I'll even up the odds again and make it two against two.'

The Detective-Inspector took off the glasses he sometimes used for reading and put them down on the desk. 'You confirm that what's written here—' he tapped a sheet of paper—'is your evidence?'

'Yes, sir,' replied Brent.

'You understand that by it you are calling Mrs Hawsley a liar?'

'Yes.'

The DI scratched the right-hand side of his neck. 'Sit down.' He turned and stared out of the window. In profile, his face gained a hint of harshness; an indication that he seldom accepted human weakness as an excuse or even a valid explanation. 'You know the Hawsleys' background?'

'Yes.'

'Such people are not in the habit of lying and making false accusations.'

'Only because they're seldom in a position to need to.'

'You envy them?'

'Perhaps. But the security they enjoy, not them as people.'

'Then it's their wealtth that you begrudge?'

'I'm sorry, but I don't see the point of the question.'

'The point is, I think you're being a fool and I'm trying to assess whether that's because you have a mistaken notion of what can be demanded in the name of friendship, or from an irrational, jealous hostility.'

'A kind of financial Red under the bed?'

'This is hardly a matter for juvenile facetiousness,' said the DI coldly. 'No policeman is asked to forgo his political opinions; every policeman is required to leave those opinions, whatever they are, at home. We are under the same duty to investigate honestly whether dealing with a down-and-out who stinks of meths or a millionaire whose aroma is Havana cigars.'

'We just have far more practice with the former.'

'You are someone who has not yet learned when it pays to keep silent.'

'Probably not, sir.'

'I've been re-reading your P and P file. You might have the makings of a good senior officer if only you could develop a stronger sense of what I'll call detached acceptance. Do you understand what I mean?'

'I think so.'

'I'll make it clear in case you choose to be mistaken. You need to develop the understanding that our job is to serve the law, not to pursue justice.'

'They're not the same thing?'

'Don't act naïve. You are very well aware that unfortunately there are times when they are not.'

'And when that happens?'

'Our duty remains quite clear. We serve the law. If that has to be changed to ensure justice, the politicians must make the change . . . In view of what I've just said, do you wish to make any alteration to your statement?'

'No, sir.'

'It is correct in every respect?'

'Yes.'

The DI put on his spectacles, picked up the sheet of paper, read. He looked up and over the tops of the spectacles. 'You were with Detective-Sergeant O'Connor from the moment he entered the house?'

'Yes.'

'And at first Mrs Hawsley was not present?'

'She did not arrive until after the sarge had found the sachet of powder.'

'Through her lawyer, she states quite categorically that she was present throughout the interview and that you were outside the house at the time of the alleged finding.'

'She's lying.'

'Yet if she is not, you are.'

'Why should I?'

'I understand that you're a personal friend of Sergeant O'Connor?'

'As a police officer, I would never let my personal feelings interfere with my duties.'

'Insolence will hardly help your case. Where was the powder found?'

'In the right-hand coat pocket of Mr Hawsley.'

'Doesn't it strike you as odd that, knowing it was there, Mr Hawsley should have agreed to being searched?'

'He was in such a muck-sweat that he'd obviously forgotten it was.'

'Does a man in a muck-sweat give a valid permission to search?'

'He did.'

'Mrs Hawsley swears her husband is not and never has been an addict. Assuming he's clean, why should he be carrying around on his person a single sachet?'

'Perhaps it was a sample, to prove the quality of what he was offering.'

'A damnfool risk to take when he was at home and wouldn't be trying to trade.'

'He's hardly a professional.'

'Precisely. In fact, almost as far from a professional drug peddler as one could get . . . What proof is there that he is or has been in any way connected with drugs?'

'He was fingered by a grasser; the grasser was murdered.'

'Until it can be proved that the act of grassing was the motive for his murder, that is proof of nothing.'

'The woman he met at the pub has been in drugs.'

'According to her record, Maureen Lewis has also been on the game. How do you know which of her occupations it was that attracted him?'

'With her looks, it has to be drugs.'

'When you are more experienced, you'll realize the fallacy of that.'

O'Connor had said the same thing, if in different terms. 'Maybe, apart from the powder that was on him, there isn't much hard legal proof that he's in drugs . . .'

'There isn't any.'

'But I'll bet anything you like that if he sees himself in real danger of facing a stiff jail sentence for possession, he'll talk hard and fast and convict himself.'

'Which brings us back to the beginning. If Sergeant

O'Connor was stupid enough, no matter what his motives, to try to plant drugs on Mr Hawsley, he will be charged with the criminal offence. Anyone who knowingly supports his false evidence will also be charged and, similarly, the motive for his actions cannot militate against his guilt, even if it might perhaps be used in mitigation of sentence. You understand that?'

'Yes, sir.'

'There will be a full investigation into Mrs Hawsley's allegations, conducted by a senior officer from another division. While that investigation is under way and until its findings are known, I have no course left open to me other than to suspend you, as I have the Detective-Sergeant, on full pay. That's all.'

Brent went over to the door, half-opened this, paused. 'There's one thing I'd like to know for sure.'

'What's that?'

'Does the word of an impoverished detective-constable carry half as much weight as a rich man's, or even less?'

'Get out,' said the DI, with angry annoyance.

CHAPTER 11

The telephone was ringing as Brent let himself into Grangeway. He hurried across the hall and picked up the receiver.

O'Connor said, his anxiety obvious: 'Where have you been? I've been trying to get hold of you for hours.'

'I had to see the old man. He kept me waiting.'

'What did he say to you?'

'Condemned my politics, objected to my insolent manner, called me a liar, and suspended me, but otherwise was quite friendly.'

'Then you didn't recant?'

'What kind of a bloody fairweather friend d'you think I am?'

'I'm sorry, Jim . . . But I've been going crazy, waiting and waiting and knowing that if you went back on what you'd said before, I'd lose everything; the house, the job, the pension . . .'

Despite himself, Brent felt momentarily scornful of O'Connor's weak self-pity. 'I said I'd back you up, didn't I?'

'Yes, I know, but . . . Did the old man believe you?'

'I told you, he called me a liar.'

'What's going to happen?'

'Brass is being called in from one of the other divisions to carry out an investigation.'

'What can we do?'

'Stick to the last comma of our story so that it remains their word against ours. Then whoever's doing the investigation can think what he likes, but if he can't actually prove anything there's nothing he can do and we'll have to be reinstated. It's the reverse side of what's been going on— knowing Hawsley has to be mixed up with drugs, but not being able to do anything about it. So provided no one plants evidence on us, we'll be all right.'

'Who'd do that?'

'No call to take to the lifeboats, I was only making a funny.'

There was a pause. 'How can you joke about it?' asked O'Connor resentfully.

'It keeps me from wondering how easy it is to cut one's throat.'

'Then you don't really think we'll get away with it?'

'All I think is, the old man was right, I do talk too much. Listen, if we stick together, don't panic, don't fall for any soft/hard approach by the brass during the investigation, we'll end up Persil white on the records.'

'Christ, I hope you're right . . . I haven't told Pam yet

what's happened. Just said I'd managed to wangle a bit of time off and that's why I was at home. But I can't go on and on saying that. And then I'll have to tell her I've been suspended and she'll be sick with worry . . .'

Brent stopped listening. Consequences could make far greater cowards of people than consciences. Fear of losing the even life he'd built up for his family had, in so little time, changed the detective-sergeant into a weak and frightened man . . .

Ironically, it was silence which brought Brent's attention back to the call. Breaking it, he said: 'Just remember one more thing. The Force won't want another scandal, not after the one three months ago in D Division. So if the investigating officer can find sufficient justification not to find us guilty, he's going to grab it . . .'

He said goodbye, replaced the receiver. Some of what he'd said had been fact, some had been wishful thinking. The investigating officer might easily be like the DI, some- one who held that the truth must be pursued, no matter at what cost . . . He went through to the larder and poured himself a gin and tonic. As he capped the tonic, he heard the front door. Susan called out: 'Jim, where are you?'

He returned to the hall. She had moved into an elegant phase. She had had a facial the previous day, her hair had been done that morning, and she was wearing a new coat that could have cost more than he earned in a year. 'You look good enough to eat.'

'Tastings only allowed; cannibalism is far too permanent . . . What are you doing here at this time of the day, boozing?'

'Getting drunk, of course.'

'Didn't your mother ever tell you that it's bad form to get drunk on your own?'

'She didn't know such a thing was possible. What can I get you to ease you on the road to perdition?'

'The same as you, if that's a G and T. Better, give me yours and go and get yourself another.'

He poured out a second drink and carried it through to the sitting-room. She was on the settee, legs tucked under her, skirt riding high up her thighs. She saw his expression. 'You're being lecherous.'

'Is that so surprising?'

'I hope not. Why d'you think I've gone to all the trouble of spending hours at the hairdresser's?'

'To satisfy yourself, not me.'

'Pig! . . . Now tell me why you're here and not at your boring job?'

'I've been suspended.'

'From what?'

'From work, of course.'

'Are you saying you've been chucked out?'

'There's been a complaint against me which has to be investigated and until it is I'm officially not a fit and proper person to continue my work.'

'The bastards!'

He was surprised by the vehemence with which she spoke.

'And you're just sitting there, letting them get away with it? Phone Thompson and tell him to create hell.'

'Who's Thompson?'

'Chris's solicitor in London. Chris says he's so sharp he's worth the hundred quid an hour he charges. Or maybe it's two hundred.'

'That is rather an important point.'

'Why? Chris will stick the fees down to one of his companies.'

'Excuse my naïveté.'

'So go and phone Thompson—his number's in my book in the telephone drawer.'

He did not move. 'I don't think it's a very good idea.'

'Why not?'

'For the moment, it would be best to let things take their course.'

She shrugged her shoulders.

He drank slowly. He experienced a growing sense of guilt, for a reason that would engage Susan's scorn. O'Connor had been devastated by the suspension, but he was relatively unconcerned by it. The difference was explained by the privileged ground on to which he'd moved. If they were discharged by the force—a penalty they could suffer if their guilt were determined, but without the degree of proof necessary for a criminal action—O'Connor would be left incomeless, pensionless, and with little possibility of ever finding a decent job. He, on the other hand, would have no such worries. Susan would keep the house going until her father found him a far better paid job . . .

She lit another cigarette. As he watched her manœuvre the long holder, he thought that in the 'twenties she would have been one of the thrill-seeking flappers, driving naked through London for a bet, never seeing the street musicians who couldn't play very well because their training had been in the trenches . . .

'Why are you looking like God when He stubs His big toe?' she asked.

'I was thinking that there's a 'twenties flapper look about you.'

'You know how to be a real sod, don't you! Can't you begin to recognize style when you see it? . . . Get me another drink.' She held out her glass. 'Exactly why have you been suspended?'

'Because I'm suspected, along with Hugh, of attempting to subvert the course of justice,' he replied as he took the glass from her.

'Hugh hasn't got it in him to subvert a two-year-old's birthday party.'

'He has hidden depths.'

'Too hidden for the rest of us to see. So what happens next?'

'There'll be an internal investigation and if that turns up sufficient proof, we'll be charged.'

'As if you were a common criminal?'

'If convicted, that's precisely what we'll become.'

'They bloody well can't do that to you.'

'There's no call to panic over what the fashionable woman wears when she visits her man in jail. Provided Hugh keeps his nerve, we'll escape.'

'It's all his fault, isn't it?'

'Why d'you say that?'

'Because I'll bet a fortune it was his mess and you rushed in to support him when you didn't need to begin to.'

It was not the first time that he had been astonished by the sharpness of her intuition. 'He's a friend.'

'And that's cause enough to risk going to jail?'

'You don't think it ever could be?'

'Being emotionally mature, I know it can't.'

'It'll all blow over, so there's no need to get your knickers in a twist.'

'Are they really twisted?'

'How would I know?'

'By looking, of course.'

CHAPTER 12

The files, filing cabinets, seldom used reference books, and old logs, which had been stored in the room beyond the DI's had been moved and replaced with a desk, two chairs, and an adjustable desk light which was old enough frequently to adjust itself. In the small brass-holder on the outside of the door a card had been inserted on which had been typed 'Officer-in-charge, Internal inquiry'. The card was the first thing that Detective Chief Superintendent Jennings changed. He tore it up.

He had the general appearance of a cheerful out-of-doors man who was good at leaning on a five-bar gate and staring at pigs rooting for acorns. Only his eyes betrayed the fact that he was no genial Farmer Giles; they were light blue and usually held a hard, questioning expression.

In old-fashioned terms, he had come up in the world the hard way. His father had died when he was only months old, his mother had had poor health and had not been able to work full time, and he had had two sisters and a brother. Money had always been very short and they had lived in a part of town where a missing face was automatically assumed to have disappeared to jail. In his early teens, he could easily have become a tough, streetwise kid who would inevitably graduate up the ladder of crime, but he'd been fortunate enough to be befriended by a policeman who had believed that it was the more important part of his job to lead a youngster away from crime than to arrest him once he'd committed it. PC Appleby. PC Plod would have been a contemporary nickname. Kind yet adhering to strict principles, slow to act, unambitious, PC Appleby had instilled in him a respect for the rights of the individual and a dislike for anyone who tried to dilute or destroy those rights; the knowledge that there was an infinite number of shades of grey between black and white; and a sense of loyalty towards the police force that was as strong as any subaltern's for his regiment. It was inevitable that Fawcus and he should find they had little in common. He looked beyond the rule book whenever there was something to be gained by doing so, Fawcus did not.

'It's a very unfortunate situation, especially following that incident in D Division a few months ago,' said the DI, an expression of irritation on his long, thin face. 'But after the complaint was made I had no option other than to do what I have.'

Jennings, coat off and bright red braces showing, fingered the newly grown, bristly moustache which his wife so disliked. 'What more have you done about finding the Lewis woman?'

'Nothing, beyond confirming that she has disappeared from all her usual haunts.'

'Find her and get her to admit that Hawsley is mixed up in drugs and his denial that the sachet was ever in his possession would look very much weaker.'

'But since it was probably planted on him . . .'

'You assume that?'

'I'd say that it's fairly certain.'

'You prefer Hawsley's and his wife's evidence to that of your own men?'

The DI flushed. 'I'm taking into account the characters of the two men concerned.'

'Which are?'

'Sergeant O'Connor is inclined to become emotionally involved in a case.'

'Is that a polite way of saying that he becomes too keen to arrest a man whom he's certain is guilty?'

'Yes.'

'There are surely worse faults in a police officer?'

'With respect, not if he is tempted to go beyond his remit.'

'His remit?' Jennings repeated the words as if savouring their flavour.

The DI said, his tone annoyed: 'Worse faults, if he's tempted to fake the evidence.'

'You've never been tempted?'

'Certainly not.'

Jennings leaned back in the chair until it was resting on its back legs; he looked his thumbs inside his braces. 'And what about DC Brent?'

'He takes his work far too casually.'

'A good officer must always take his work seriously?'

'In my opinion, yes. In addition, Brent is ever ready to allow the dictates of friendship to override all others.'

'It sounds as if he makes for a good companion.'

'But not always a good police officer.'

'I wish I could be as certain as you obviously are as to

which is the more important . . . How far have you checked
out Hawsley?'

'We've discovered nothing to connect him with the drug
scene.'

'But you have thoroughly investigated his background?'

'Not in any depth. It's unfortunate that the detective-
sergeant's contact was murdered—'

'Which suggests his information was correct.'

'There's nothing to say that Wallace was murdered because he'd been grassing on Hawsley. It may be because he
was grassing on someone else.'

'Yet if you could prove a definite tie-in, it would go a long
way to destroying the evidence against your two men.'

'If Sergeant O'Connor did attempt to plant the evidence,
that's that.'

'You wouldn't try to find something that might begin to
excuse his actions—always assuming that he did act?'

The DI was silent.

'Then we've covered as much ground as I want to for the
moment. So now we'll reactivate the investigations into the
present whereabouts of Maureen Lewis and the background
of Hawsley.'

'That will be rather heavy on manpower. I've far more
work in hand than I can reasonably cope with as it is.'

'Show me a divisional DI who doesn't and I'll show you
a man who's not doing his full job.'

'What I'm trying to say, sir, is that the whereabouts of
Maureen Lewis and the nature of Hawsley's background
have no direct connection with whether Detective-Sergeant
O'Connor attempted to plant evidence on Hawsley and
Detective-Constable Brent is hoping to protect him by lying.'

'And what I've been trying to point out is that if we can
prove that Hawsley is into drugs, the question of planted
evidence becomes of very much less consequence.'

'In my opinion, it would alter very little, if indeed it
altered anything at all.'

Jennings released his thumbs, letting the braces snap back on to his chest. He tipped the chair forward until it was on all four legs, rested his elbows on the desk. 'I've been appointed to be in charge of the investigations into the allegation of an attempted perversion of justice and in my opinion the inquiries I've outlined are central to the matter. You'll therefore second two DCs to my command right away and, if it proves necessary, I'll have a couple of PCs added later on.'

The DI's expression was one of angry rebellion, but his words were those of a man who always accepted the commands of rank. 'Very well, sir.'

Jennings studied the PC as he walked from the doorway to the chair. 'Joe Marks?'

'That's right, sir.'

'Sit down . . . You were on night turn in Property on Tuesday, the twenty-fourth?'

'Yes, sir.'

Jennings opened one of the two ledgers on the desk and checked through the pages, as if having to search for what he wanted. Time could often unsettle an interviewee. 'Are the entries concerning access correct?'

'Yes, sir.'

'No officer entered Property without signing? Take your time to answer and remember that it will be on record.' Although he spoke pleasantly, he made it quite clear that he was convinced there had been an omission.

The PC's memory had been jogged and although he liked O'Connor, he hastily accepted that this was a case where he had to look after his own interests by covering himself. 'As a matter of fact, sir, there was someone who entered Property, but didn't sign.'

'Who was that?'

'Detective-Sergeant O'Connor.'

'Why didn't you make certain he signed?'

'I had a lot of cataloguing to do and was very busy and just . . . Well, kind of thought he'd do it without me telling him.'

'Did Sergeant O'Connor also open the strongbox although he didn't sign that log book either?'

'Yes, sir. I'm afraid I slipped up again.'

'It would be more exact to say you fell flat on your face . . . What did he want?'

'As I recall, he thought there'd been a fresh drug bust and he wanted to check what was on ice.'

'Did he put anything into, or bring anything out of, the strongbox?'

'I can't really say, sir.'

'Too busy to do your job?'

In a spirit of antagonism, Marks said: 'As far as I could judge, he didn't.'

'I don't think your judgement has much of a foundation . . . That's all.'

O'Connor would have made a poor criminal, Jennings decided. He was trying so hard to portray a man at peace with his conscience that he looked as guilty as hell. 'You were both in the house from the time of your arrival to the time of your departure?'

'Yes, sir.'

'And Mrs Hawsley was not present until after you found the sachet of powder?'

'She wasn't, no.'

'You maintain that she's a liar?'

'If she says that she was present when I found it, yes, sir.'

'You did not take the sachet with you to the house in order to plant it on Mr Hawsley?'

'No, sir.'

'Suppose you had done that, what would have been your motive?'

The question perplexed O'Connor, already perplexed by

the Detective Chief Superintendent's easy, pleasant manner.

'You don't like hypothetical questions? Then answer one that's more concrete. Do you personally know anyone who has become a drug addict in recent months?'

'I . . .'

'You do?'

'The son of friends of ours.'

'That sort of contact makes one really understand the terrible dangers of the trade, doesn't it?'

'Yes, it does . . .' O'Connor stopped, realizing too late that the question might have been a trap, in which case his answer had dropped him right into it. But the Detective Chief Superintendent's expression showed only understanding, not any sense of triumph.

'Why should I want to change my evidence?' Brent demanded, with reckless antagonism.

'Perhaps because you've decided it might be best for all concerned, not least yourself, to tell the truth,' replied Jennings with surprising patience, considering he was a man whose temper was usually on a fairly short fuse.

'I have told the truth. Mrs Hawsley was not present when the powder was found, as she claims. Sergeant O'Connor found the sachet in Mr Hawsley's pocket and did not try to plant it there.'

'You can swear he didn't?'

'Yes.'

'Were you watching him that closely?'

'Yes.'

'Why?'

'Because it's a rule to do so when another officer is searching a suspect.'

'And you are a man who always observes the rules?'

Brent didn't know how to answer that ironic question.

'Have you known Sergeant O'Connor for long?'

'Since I came to the division, just over three years ago.'

'And in those three years you have become a personal friend of his?'

'I am not lying because of that.'

'You haven't answered the question.'

'Yes, he's a friend.'

'Thank you. That's all.'

Bewildered by this sudden ending of a brief questioning—he had expected it to last far longer and to be far more searching—Brent left.

Like many people, Jennings thought, Brent's character contained elements which could appear to be in direct conflict. At times he mocked or resented authority and obligations, yet he was prepared to risk everything to honour a sense of personal loyalty.

CHAPTER 13

At twenty-five, DC Adams was already beginning to bald. He met the jeering references to approaching senility from his fellow detectives with the assertion that yes, it was true, premature baldness was a sign of impressive virility.

Jennings walked round to the chair behind the desk, sat. 'Well?'

'I'm afraid it's a negative report, sir.'

'You can't find any trace at all of the woman?'

'So far, there's not a whisper of her whereabouts.'

'Then she might well have been murdered?'

'There's nothing to say she has been, nothing to say she hasn't.'

'What have you been able to dig up on her recent background?'

'Not very much. She was in the roving stud game—running three or four girls who worked the hotels and motels—but suddenly gave that up. There's a blank before she was busted for drugs and it's blank again since then. No one knows who she's been working with.'

'Or they won't say?'

'That's more than likely. None of my usual contacts likes talking about her.'

Jennings fiddled with his moustache. 'If I'd heard what happened to Wallace, I don't suppose I'd be keen to talk . . . Carry on and keep digging.'

'Frankly, sir, I don't think there's anything more I can usefully do.'

'On the contrary, you can keep digging.'

Adams mentally shrugged his shoulders, left.

Jennings picked up the typewritten statement on top of the papers on his desk and read it. DC Williams had investigated Hawsley's background as far as possible while working to discreet standards. Hawsley was an accountant who had been at Asteys, a financial firm in the City which had expanded into the conglomerate it now was. A couple of years back, he'd left them to work for the Seetonhurst Wine Company, which imported wines and spirits from Spain.

His wife's maiden name was Derales; the Derales claimed direct descent from one of the barons who had come over with William the Conqueror. Among the locals she was not liked, being labelled a snob. She was chairman of the parish council and by reputation an aggressive, abrasive one, yet even those who criticized her had to admit that she got things done.

No hint anywhere of any connection with the drug trade. He dropped the paper, stood, walked over to the window and looked out at the sun-splashed roofs. On the face of things, here were a fairly prosperous, middle-aged, middle-class couple; people who'd even think twice about pocketing a pound coin they found in the street. Yet O'Connor's contact had named Hawsley as being in the drug trade, that contact had been murdered; Hawsley had met Maureen

Lewis, one-time prostitute, one-time madam, whose last conviction had been for a drug-related offence . . .

He put his hands in his pockets and fiddled with some coins in the right-hand one. As the DI had pointed out, these inquiries had no immediate bearing on whether the two detectives had attempted to pervert the course of justice. It could be said that by ordering them he had been guilty of wasting time and manpower. Yet if he concentrated solely on the question of whether or not the detective-sergeant had attempted to plant a sachet of drugs on Hawsley, he was going to have to order that the contents of that sachet be analysed and compared with the contents of the others in the strongbox—and he hadn't the slightest doubt that similarities would be found which would go a long way towards proving that the Detective-Sergeant had set out falsely to incriminate Hawsley . . .

No matter how jealous he was of the Force's reputation, he would never fake the results of an investigation. But since time could produce unexpected bonuses, he saw no reason not to prolong that investigation.

DC Williams spoke to Mrs Halford in the garden behind her cottage. She was a small woman with a tremendous energy which had not been sapped by raising a family of four rumbustious boys. Unable to remain still for very long, she repeatedly bent down to pull out a blade of grass or a spike of bindweed that had inadvisably appeared in the herbaceous border. 'I had to go to the annual general meeting even though Alf always has a moan when I leave him on his own. You'd think I was away for a month and leaving him to do all the housework. But as I tell him, someone in the parish has to see things get done.' She suddenly and for no apparent reason walked past the border and down a grass path to the immaculately maintained kitchen garden. She pointed at several staked tomato plants which carried trusses of yellow tomatoes. 'D'you know them?'

'I can't say I do.'

'Golden Wonder. Got all the flavour tomatoes used to have before the supermarkets wanted 'em the same shape and size, never mind what they taste like. I grow all our own vegetables. What about you?'

He weeded his two flowerbeds only with the greatest reluctance and when his wife badgered him more than usual, but it was a tenet of every good interrogator to share any declared enthusiasm. 'I do what I can, but I don't really have the time.'

'It takes time, all right. But as I've always said, if you need time, you can make it.' She moved along the row, nipping out side shoots. 'There's one that's ripe. Try it and say if you've ever eaten one with more flavour.'

He picked the large yellow tomato and bit into it. Warmed by the sun, almost as sweet as sugar, it was filled with the taste which had so often become only a memory. His praise was genuine.

'All my vegetables taste like they should.'

'I'll bet they do! . . . About this meeting. I suppose Mrs Hawsley was there?'

'She's chairwoman, isn't she?'

'When did she arrive?'

'How would I know?' She chuckled. 'Me and her aren't the closest of friends. As Alf says, she keeps her nose so high up in the air, it's a wonder it doesn't get frozen. But I do have to say this, she gets things done and if someone needs to make a noise, she never minds making it. Not afraid of anyone.'

'At what time did the meeting start?'

'Six. On the dot.'

'So I expect you got there a little beforehand?'

'That's right.'

'Was she there when you arrived?'

'She was.'

'And naturally she was present throughout the meeting?'

'She had to leave because she'd forgotten some papers. As I said to Steve—he's also on the committee—it wasn't like her to forget things.'

'How long was she away?'

'It's funny, that is.' She bent down to pull out some groundsel which had managed to grow almost to seeding by hiding within the leaves of a tomato plant. 'She was gone so long that Steve telephoned her place to discover what was happening. He couldn't make head or tail of what she said; sounded like she was tight.' She laughed. 'Steve was only joking, of course. The likes of her don't get tight. Or if they do, they make sure no one else knows.'

'What happened with the meeting?'

'Steve said it wasn't any good waiting and we ought to start again with someone else in the chair. But then George said we couldn't do that as we'd started with her and there was a real argument. All about nothing, really, but that's men for you.'

'She didn't return?'

'Never heard another word from her.'

'When exactly did she leave the meeting?'

'I can't rightly say. I mean, I wasn't watching the clock.'

'Then have a guess.'

'I suppose it was something like a quarter of an hour after we'd started. It always takes a bit of time to quieten down and she'd read out the minutes of the last meeting and we'd agreed 'em. And it wasn't until we'd started discussing how to pay for the repairs to the village hut that she discovered she'd forgotten to bring the estimates from the three builders . . . A quarter of an hour; twenty minutes; something of that order.'

'This bloke Steve—I'd like a word with him. So what's his surname and where's he live?'

'Steven Armstrong. His place is the first one after Maiden's Copse. You can't mistake it because of the Jerseys.'

*

Williams stared with incomprehension at the five-gallon glass jars, the clusters, the vacuum lines, the pit, and the feed troughs of the herringbone milking parlour. Armstrong was a tall, rangy man, with a weatherbeaten face and a bright red 'farmer's nose'. He directed the hose at the far side of the pit and washed off a trail of dung, then turned it off. 'A real bitch, if ever I've met one,' he said, his voice heavy with the local burr.

'Mrs Halford says she had to leave the meeting after it started. What I'm trying to do is find out what sort of time that was.'

Armstrong climbed the four steps out of the pit. He untied the rubber apron, slipped the top loop over his head, hung the apron on the rails of a feeding trough. 'A quarter past six, half past. It was soon after we'd started, anyway . . . Why the interest?'

'Just checking up,' replied Williams vaguely. 'Later on you phoned her and I gather she sounded a bit strange?'

'As tight as a tick.'

'D'you think she really was drunk?'

'Her? Never.'

'Then what d'you suppose was the problem?'

'I wouldn't know. Maybe the husband had just found the courage to say no to her. Even a worm will turn.'

Jennings studied the report. O'Connor said he and Brent had arrived at Cockscomb Farm at five past six. If one accepted his time, then Mrs Hawsley could not have been present throughout that meeting and she was lying to support her husband, just as Brent was lying to support O'Connor. Unfortunately, unless all the times could be established beyond question—probably impossible—there was not sufficient proof here to shake the Hawsleys' evidence and name them liars so firmly as to destroy belief in their claims that O'Connor had tried to plant the evidence . . .

The phone rang.

'It's Adams, sir. I've just received the whisper that Maureen Lewis could be up in Smoke. I've tried for details, but even though I fed my contact enough gin to float an oil rig, she wouldn't say anything more.'

'Because she didn't know, or because she was too scared?'

'I just couldn't be certain.'

'How reliable is she?'

'I've had useful leads from her, but as many bum ones when she's been needing free booze.'

'Is there any point in getting back on to her?'

'I doubt it'll do much good, but I will if you like.'

'Have a go.'

Jennings replaced the receiver. That sounded like a lead that would lead nowhere. So it could not reasonably be held to justify any further delay in ordering an analysis of the contents of the sachets . . .

The phone rang again. A local reporter was asking about a rumour that two divisional detectives had been suspended from duty and was there any truth in this? Did the Detective Chief Superintendent want to talk to the reporter? No, he didn't, since the case needed publicity like he needed his ears cropped. But if he didn't say something, a whole catalogue of damaging misfacts would probably be printed . . . Goddamnit, why had O'Connor and Brent been such bloody fools?

CHAPTER 14

Caroline Hawsley looked across the sitting-room. 'When I was up in the village shop this morning I saw Tim Atkins. He says that Walling Hall is coming on the market soon.'

'Is it?' Hawsley was careful to sound uninterested. They might well be able to afford to move to a more imposing home, but he was intelligent enough always to have recognized that it would be dangerously foolhardy to be seen to be spending more money than was reasonably feasible. And thank God he'd observed that rule! The detectives could pry as hard as they liked, they'd find no evidence of excessive spending to confirm their suspicions . . .

'He says it's in excellent structural repair and would need only a little redecorating. The Halley-Andrews used to live there. They're a very old county family.'

He did not share her respect for old county families who had fallen on hard times.

'Climpsons are the agents. Tim says that he's heard the asking price will be around half a million. That's a reasonable price, isn't it?'

'I wouldn't know. And with the way prices have been see-sawing, I don't suppose anyone else does, either.'

'It's a beautiful park, even though it's small.'

Did she see herself in a Vanbrugh mansion in the middle of a thousand acres? He stood. 'I've some work I must finish off, so I'll go upstairs and do it . . . By the way, I have to be in London tomorrow and the next day, so I'll stay up there for a couple of nights.'

'All right.'

She never questioned his visits to London. Because she believed his explanations; because she guessed the truth, but with that strange ability of hers, shut her mind to what she guessed; because she guessed and didn't care? He walked towards the door, his mind filling with images of Maggie in all her naked voluptuousness . . .

'Ashley, I want you to ring Lampson in the morning to tell him to make another, even stronger complaint.'

He came to a stop, Maggie banished from his mind.

'A detective has been asking other members of the parish council what the times were when I arrived at the last meeting and when I left. I am not going to suffer such insolence.'

'What did they tell the police?'

'I've no idea,' she answered dismissively.

Couldn't she understand that if the police determined she had not been in the house throughout the detectives' visit, her evidence became valueless? Let that happen and he was in danger of being wrongly convicted as a drug addict and/ or peddler unless he made a full confession . . .

Susan, stretched out on a swing-seat in the shade of an oak tree, said, 'D'you know what I'd really like to do? Jump in the car, catch the ferry to Calais, drive to Marquise, and have dinner at Chez François.'

'It sounds a long way to go for a meal,' Brent observed from a deckchair.

'Their steak farci foie gras is a divine revelation.'

'Give me bangers and mash at the Black Bull.'

'You know you're not that much of a Philistine . . . Let's do it. Now.'

He shook his head.

'Don't be such a sodden blanket. Do the unexpected and life ceases to be so boring.'

'You're forgetting that I've been suspended on full pay. That means I have to be available all the time in case they want to question me.'

'Are you trying to tell me you can't even go out to see friends?'

'Not if they happen to live in France.'

'I really wish I could understand you. They kick you in the teeth and all you can do is bow and say yes, sir, no sir.'

'No backbone, that's my trouble.'

'Or is it the money you're worrying about. I'll pay.'

'No, Miss Rothschild, it's not the money, it's a sense of duty. I'll try to explain the term in simple—'

'Don't try to be bloody patronizing.'

The cordless telephone on the patio table rang. She reached out, picked it up, extended the aerial. 'Yes?'

'Are you the bleeding split's prosey?'

'What on earth do you mean?'

'If you don't want to see your Bristols chopped off, tell him he didn't see nothing.' The connection was cut.

She lowered the phone, her expression perplexed.

'Who was that?' he asked.

'Some nut making an obscene call, I suppose; except it was too incomprehensible to be obscene. Or maybe he was tight.'

'If so, he's started early in the day. What exactly did he say?'

'Something like, was I the bleeding split's prosey and if I didn't want to see my Bristols chopped off, I had to tell someone he didn't see anything . . . Can you begin to make any sense out of that?'

He tried to control his expression of shock, but clearly failed.

'You do know what he was on about?'

'Probably.'

'Then translate.'

'If you're the detective's girlfriend . . .' He became silent.

'Go on.'

'He's trying to get you to persuade me to change my evidence.'

'Well, I'm damned! . . . The bloody insolence!'

He was grateful that for the moment at least she was more concerned about the man's insolence than the vicious threat contained in his words.

Jennings stood, feet apart, hands resting on the desk as he leaned slightly forward. 'I've received the report from the county laboratory regarding the analyses of the contents of the sachets. All contained adulterated hard drugs—one lot was heroin, the other two cocaine. The cocaine in the larger pile and the single sachet came from the same source. The adulterant is the same in every sachet, but in two there is an additional level of adulteration and the added adulterant is the same. The sachet allegedly found in Mr Hawsley's possession is one of the two.' He stared at O'Connor, who stood on the right of Brent. 'Obviously, you'll understand the full significance of this.'

O'Connor gave no answer.

'One sachet was taken from the larger pile in the strong-box and this was further adulterated in order to make two sachets. The first was replaced on the larger pile, the second was used in an attempt to plant false evidence on Mr Hawsley.'

'There is another possible explanation,' said Brent.

'Which is what?'

'That the cocaine in Hawsley's possession came from the same source as the other.'

'Only the one sachet in the larger pile is doubly adulter-ated.'

'Is there proof that all the contents of the sachets in that pile were exactly similar before they were put in the strongbox?'

'No.'

'Then it looks as if the pile came from two sources and the sachet in Hawsley's possession was from the second.'

'I'm not simple,' said Jennings angrily.

'Sir, all I'm saying is—'

'Not for the first time, I suggest that it's in your interests to say nothing. My inquiry is completed and I'll be submit-ting my report to the Assistant Chief Constable. In it, I will state that it's my opinion that all four persons present at Cookscomb Farm on Thursday, the twenty-sixth of last month, are lying. Since my brief was to investigate the allegation that you, Sergeant O'Connor, attempted to plant false evidence on Mr Hawsley, I am not addressing myself to the much wider question of whether or not there is evidence that he is in any way connected with the drug trade. I have suggested that while the laboratory evidence makes it clear where some of the truth lies, it does not establish such truth beyond doubt; in other words, there is not sufficient evidence to warrant criminal proceedings, but there is for an internal disciplinary hearing. The decision on whether that will be held will be taken by the Chief Constable.' He took his hands off the desk and stood upright. He spoke to O'Connor. 'Haven't you learned enough to know that, however noble your motives, if you try to fight crime illegally, you merely breed more crime?'

O'Connor, whose expression made it clear that he recognized his career was probably ruined, stared fixedly at the far wall.

Jennings sighed. It was almost certainly true to say that although the world would be a more comfortable place if there weren't any idealists, it would be a poorer one. 'That's all.'

O'Connor turned, went over to the door, and opened this before he realized that Brent had not followed him. He looked back.

'I'd like a word with you, sir,' said Brent.

Jennings nodded. He sat, waited until O'Connor had gone out and closed the door, said: 'Well?'

'This morning there was a telephone call to home and my girlfriend answered it. The man said that if she didn't want her breasts chopped off, she'd better persuade me I didn't see anything.'

Jennings picked up a pencil and fiddled with it.

'He's saying . . .'

'I'm perfectly capable of understanding what he's saying. Was your girlfriend able to give you any details about the call which might help to identify the caller?'

'No.'

'There was no specific reference to the Hawsley case?'

'There doesn't have to be.'

'On the contrary, there does.'

'It's obvious.'

'Nothing is obvious until it's proved.'

'Hawsley is mixed up in the drug racket and those behind him are trying to frighten me into—' He stopped.

'Into telling the truth?'

'No, sir.'

'Brent, I've already made it clear that in my report I've not dealt with the broader problem of Hawsley's involvement in the drug trade. But obviously I've considered the question. The only things to support the suggestion are the word of an informer and the fact that Hawsley met a woman who has one conviction for drug-dealing. Unfortunately, neither can be questioned. He was murdered, she has disappeared.'

'Hawsley was in possession of cocaine.'

Jennings said exasperatedly: 'Don't you ever listen, even to common sense? What firm evidence there is suggests that he is not connected with drugs. He leads a normal, ordinary life in which there are no signs of excessive spending. He has a job with a local firm which is expanding. He has no known criminal associates . . . And spare me your objection about the Lewis woman. Although the facts suggest the meeting was prearranged, there's no proof that it was; still less is there any proof that the subject of their discussion was drugs rather than sex. If he went on trial tomorrow, the jury would see him as a decent citizen. Accepting that, it's impossible to make the assumption that he was in any way connected with the threat to your girlfriend.'

'I don't give a damn for all the ifs, buts, and maybes, I want her protected.'

'You're asking for police protection on the grounds of one telephone call from an unknown man with an unknown motive? You must know that's impossible.'

'Just because you think I'm lying my head off to help the sarge—'

Jennings sharply interrupted. 'That has nothing to do with it. I'm treating your request—which, of course, should have been made to your DI—exactly as I would had it come from a member of the public. I shouldn't have to point out that to provide round-the-clock protection to an individual calls for a very considerable commitment of manpower; manpower which is needed in half a dozen other places. Which is why it's only provided when a need is definitely identified.'

'And you say that it isn't?'

'Until one can be quite certain that Hawsley is engaged in the drug trade, it can't be.'

'When I was at training college, they told me that the police were a team. Some team!'

Jennings said: 'If you can prove, and I mean prove, that she is in danger because of the case, put an official request for protection through your DI. He will forward that to county HQ for approval and I will make certain that approval is granted immediately.'

Brent muttered his thanks, recognizing despite his bitter anger that in all the circumstances it was a generous offer.

CHAPTER 15

The phone rang at 11.15 on Thursday morning, as Susan and Brent were about to leave the house and drive over to Mereton Hall where they were to have lunch. 'I'll go,' she said. 'It may be Joanna.'

He carried on outside, to stand in the warm sunshine. If the caller were Joanna, he'd a long wait ahead of him . . . There was a shout and he returned inside. She was standing with the receiver in her right hand, an expression of shock on her face. His first thought was that something had happened to one of her immediate family 'Is someone ill?'

She didn't answer.

He took hold of her arms. 'Susie, love, what's happened?'

She made a whimpering sound.

'Is it your father? Has your mother had an accident?'

'Oh God! I want to be sick.' She slammed the receiver down. 'Because of you, they're going to . . .' She shivered.

He realized this had been a second threatening call from the drugs mob. 'Was it the same man as yesterday?'

'He told me exactly what he and his friends will do to me. Oh God, I didn't know anyone could think of such filthy, disgusting things.'

Even in the middle of his sharp concern, he was surprised that someone as sophisticated as she liked to think herself could be quite so shocked by the obscenities of which man was capable. 'I know it's horrible, but . . .'

'You don't know a bloody thing. You don't begin to know what it's like to be a woman and to have a man tell you all the revolting things he's going to do to your body. You probably don't even care. All's fun and fair in sex. Maybe you'd even like to join in—'

'Pull yourself together.'

His harsh words stemmed her panic.

'Susie, what they're trying to do is to frighten you. They'll never carry out their threats.' But he remembered the attractive woman of twenty-two who'd died in the middle of telling him what her rapist had done to her.

'If you'd heard him, you wouldn't be so confident.'

'Tell me precisely what he did say.' He waited. But it became clear that she, who so often said whatever she judged would be most likely to shock her listener, could not easily bring herself to repeat the words. 'We need a good strong drink.'

She followed him in and watched him pour out two whiskies. They drank in the kitchen, standing by the table.

'What did the man say?' he asked a second time.

'That unless you tell the truth, they'll . . . they'll do all those ghastly things to me.'

'Those were his exact words—unless I tell the truth?'

'I don't know. I'm not a bloody tape-recorder. Why's he

allowed to go free? Why don't you arrest the filthy swine?'

He let her talk wildly on. In the caller's words was confirmation—should anyone still need it—that the threatening calls were directly connected with Hawsley. Only Hawsley, his wife, O'Connor, and himself, could be certain that the police evidence was a lie . . . The men running this mob had already proved themselves to be utterly brutal and if they thought it would gain them an advantage, they'd subject Susan to all the vile acts they'd threatened. In his mind's eye, he saw her, disgustingly abused, and he knew a violent, surging anger . . . He forced the picture away. 'Have another drink.'

For a moment, it seemed she had not heard him because she made no response, then she held out her glass. 'Could . . . could they really do such ghastly things?'

'No. But they're trying to scare you into believing they could.' He took her glass and went into the larder.

She came and stood in the doorway. 'Terrible sex crimes do happen. They're in the papers every day.'

'Look, you're not on your own; I'm here. If any of them tries to show his ugly nose, I'll flatten the bastard.'

Mereton Hall was late Georgian, set well back from the lane within a two-acre garden, partially walled, which was kept trim and colourful by one full-time and one part-time gardener. Radford was cheerful, welcoming, and very adept at concealing the hard, ambitious man he was; Veronica was tall, slim, attractively keeping age at bay by expensive means, and vague. Brent had never been able to determine whether they were pleasant to him because they liked or disliked him.

Radford checked the time. 'I'd better start making a move since I have to be at Heathrow at five. But I'll see you again before you go, won't I? You're not off just yet?'

'No, we're not,' Brent replied.

'Good.' He stood. He was wearing a lightweight suit

which did not need a label to identify itself as Savile Row.

'I'll come up and make certain you've everything you need,' said Veronica.

They left through the far doorway in the long dining-room which had an intricate parget ceiling. A moment later Mrs Weston, the daily, came in to clear the table. Susan led the way through the second doorway into the smaller drawing-room and settled on the chesterfield. 'D'you want a liqueur?'

'That sounds an excellent idea,' he replied.

'You know where everything's kept. Can I have a maraschino, please.'

Drinks were kept in a large cupboard that was concealed by oak panelling. He poured her out a maraschino and himself an armagnac, a liqueur to which she had introduced him.

She thanked him as he handed her her glass, sipped the drink, looked at him as he sat. 'Jim, would you mind too terribly if I didn't return to Grangeway tonight? I'm sorry, but that telephone call's really scared me. I know you say that that's all the man wanted to do and that he'd never carry out any of the filthy things he said, but . . . I just can't face being there for a while.'

'But if I'm there, nothing can—'

She interrupted him, her voice sharpening. 'You didn't hear what that filthy beast said and the ghastly relish with which he said it.'

Her recent calmness was obviously more fragile than he'd thought. 'There's no hassle, then. I'll ring the station to give them this number and they can get hold of me if they need to. There's one thing, you can feel a hundred and one per cent safe here with all the alarms and two Rottweilers to take chunks out of anyone foolhardy enough to argue with them.'

'It'll be better if I'm on my own. Just for the few days.'

'Why?'

'Veronica can be very stuffy. She wouldn't like your sleeping here.'

'She what? Does she think I leave Grangeway as soon as it gets dark every night?'

'Please understand and don't make things more difficult than they are. I'll make it up to you later on.'

He realized that there was nothing to be gained by arguing. 'Is that a promise?'

'Cross my heart and hope to—' She stopped abruptly, frightened by the ending of the saying.

Brent wondered how anyone could have been so stupid as to waste time and money making the film just shown on TV, then wondered how he could have been so stupid as to watch it right through. He switched off the set and the silence closed in on him. It needed two people to keep a house alive.

Did he have another drink, knowing he'd already had more than enough? Yes, he bloody well did. He needed something to keep the blues at bay. Goddamnit, women could make a strong man weak without bothering to cut off his hair . . .

The final drink drunk, the downstairs locked up, he climbed the stairs. The air in the bedroom was tinged with Surprise, her scent. He visualized her in bed, calling on him to hurry and undress . . .

Once in bed, he opened the paperback he'd started the night before. The hero flattered a lady who, quite clearly, was soon going to prove she was no lady . . . He dropped the book on to the bedside table, switched off the light.

The room drifted sideways, steadied up, drifted again. Experience suggested that if he'd had one more whisky, by now the room would have been lurching . . .

Drink had a strange effect on his sleeping pattern. If he'd had more than normal, but not enough to become drunk, then invariably he woke up during the night and could not quickly get back to sleep, thus giving himself plenty of time in which to wonder why in hell he hadn't either drunk less or more.

He'd been awake seemingly for hours and was beginning finally to drift back to sleep when a sound irritatingly jerked him back to full wakefulness. A door, left ajar, gently banging in a draught? But all downstairs windows were closed. He listened intently. There was silence inside the house and only the muted noise of occasional traffic from outside.

He ceased to listen and composed himself for sleep, but his mind had been stimulated and now was not ready to be turned off. How long was Susan going to remain at Mereton? Why did it have to be so bitter an experience to reach under the bedclothes and feel only space? He'd always prided himself on being self-sufficient, yet here he was, missing her as desperately as a teenager missing his first love . . .

There was another sound, which seemed to have come from nearer. Another door? But draughts called for wind and in the slightest wind the leaves of the Virginia creeper outside the bedroom rustled . . . And then he realized something that should have been clear from the beginning. He was hearing the sounds of someone inside the house.

His first reaction was one of satisfaction because here was a chance to work off some of his sense of angry frustration. The intruder (or intruders) would believe that surprise was on his side; he was about to be surprised. A weapon? In one of the cupboards were a pair of Indian clubs. He swivelled round in the bed as he folded back the sheet and single blanket, put his feet on the carpeted floor, stood. He roughly fixed the pillows and bedclothes to suggest two sleeping forms, left the bed and crossed to the last built-in cupboard by the window, moving silently. He reached inside and brought out one of the clubs. Balanced, heavy, it would make a good cosh.

On a job like this, there would probably be more than one man; two, perhaps even three. They could not know the layout of the house, so would have to have some sort of light. The sophisticated villains were using image intensifiers, but he doubted that heavies on a routine job would enjoy such advanced equipment; much more likely a torch with most of the bowl blanked off. A small spot of light left a lot of surrounding darkness. He crossed the bedroom into the en-suite bathroom. By the handbasin were a number of aerosols and bottles, dedicated to making Susan look nice and smell sweet. He picked up three aerosols and carried these through to the bedroom where, measuring by touch, he set them down on the floor just beyond the arc that the door would trace out as it was opened.

He stood by the lock side of the door to be by the light switch. Their backs would be to him and surprise would give him the seconds he needed . . .

He caught further sounds of movement, but couldn't judge whether it was the swish of clothing or shoes on a carpet; whichever, they had reached the landing. Faced with four doors to their right and three to their left, plus linen cupboards, they'd check each room in turn to discover which was the occupied one. He gripped the club more firmly and made a practice swing through the dark.

Another sound, from much closer. He adjusted his balance. Any minute now, they'd turn the door handle very slowly . . . The door opened, so quietly that it could never have woken him had he been asleep. There was a brief pause. A torch was switched on and the beam crossed to the bed. In the very poor light, the pillows made it look as if there were two people asleep. Satisfied all was quiet, they moved forward . . . They stepped on the aerosols and as their feet rolled away from under themselves, they fell, cursing wildly.

He switched on the centre light. There were four men, not two or three, wearing ski-masks. Two were sprawled on the floor, a third, lucky enough to have stepped clear of the cans, was to the right of them, and the fourth was still in the doorway.

Four to one, even with two momentarily out of action, were bitter odds. He swung the club into the fourth man's face and the man doubled up, to the accompaniment of strange bubbling noises, a hand already clasped to his mouth. The third man, torch in his left hand, reacting far more quickly than Brent would have wished, drew a knife, holding it slightly in front of himself at waist level—the stance of an experienced knife-fighter. Brent moved the club as if to aim for the man's head but then, as the other leaned back to take his head out of range, altered the direction of the swing to smash the club down on the right wrist. The knife went flying.

The two who'd been on the floor were coming to their feet. One held a torch, the other an automatic. Brent lunged forward and jabbed the end of the club into the face of the man with a gun. The man cried out. Brent slammed the club down on to his hand, but failed to knock the automatic free. He moved to make a second and more effective blow, and trod on one of the aerosols. Despite wild efforts to maintain his balance, he went flying.

The man with the gun was firmly on his feet and beginning to take aim. Brent scrambled up, expecting any second to feel the tearing impact of a bullet, but this didn't happen. A fleeting glance suggested that the gunman had been unable to fire because although the blow had not been squarely delivered, his trigger finger had been broken.

The gunman's companion, who'd stood aside to allow a clear aim, came in, knife in his right hand. He flipped the knife to his left hand just before he aimed a slashing blow. Brent jerked backwards and the knife just missed. As he moved to his right, to escape the next attack, a blow temporarily numbed his left shoulder and then filled it with fire. He dropped to the ground, rolled over, and swept the club round even though he had no definite target. It caught a man in the back of the leg and the other fell sideways against a wall.

A toecap raked his cheek. He rolled over once more, but towards his latest assailant and not away, and brought the club up to catch the man in the groin. The man collapsed, gagging. Brent stood. The man with the broken finger was still trying to ease the gun free so that he could either use another finger or pass it to a companion. Unable to cross the distance between them in time, Brent did the only thing left to him—he threw the club. It began to revolve as it cut through the air and the base came round to smash into the man's already injured face.

He threw himself forward to get hold of the club and one of them moved to cut him off. With no chance of reaching the club, he changed direction. He grabbed the muzzle of the automatic and twisted. The man shuddered and then screamed. The gun did not come free. Brent was aware of movement to his right and instinctively ducked. The blade of a knife sliced across his neck. He pulled and swung on the gun, bringing the screaming man round and into his latest assailant, upsetting a second thrust so that the blade cut his pyjama trousers but not his flesh. One more violent wrench and he finally freed the gun. He jumped back.

They ran, each man now intent only on saving himself and careless of the fate of his companions. Two of them became jammed together in the doorway, to provide a flavour of farce as each tried to force his way through.

He raised the automatic and took aim. Certain that if they'd had the chance, they'd have murdered him, he knew a fierce desire to pull the trigger, but somehow he found—and despised himself for finding—sufficient self-control not to do so. To shoot someone who was trying to escape, whatever had been that person's intentions, was illegal. British law liked to favour the criminal, not the victim.

CHAPTER 16

Detective-Inspector Fawcus took off his glasses and put them on the desk. He said: 'These men didn't suggest what their motive was?'

'They didn't say a single word from beginning to end,' replied Brent.

'So there can be no certainty that their break-in was directly connected with the threats which Miss Radford has been receiving.'

'For Pete's sake—'

'I said, no certainty.'

'You have to be as thick as two planks to believe that.'

'There is no need to be insolent.'

'No? Not when I asked for protection for her and the chief super refused it? Not when it's only luck and the fact that she was too scared to sleep at Grangeway that she isn't in hospital or the mortuary right now?'

'Part of my job is to make certain I do not respond to emotion. Let me repeat, on what you've told me, there is no certainty that the break-in followed on the telephone calls and was a direct consequence of the Hawsley case. On the present evidence, there would be a high probability of that if, and only if, it could be proved that Mr Hawsley had connections with the drug trade.'

'So were four men, armed with knives and at least one gun, just looking around for whatever took their fancy?'

'Regrettably, that happens.'

'What are you really saying? That you still refuse to protect her? Mr Jennings said—'

'He told me precisely what he said. The decision whether to pass on a request for twenty-four-hour protection has to be mine; the facts of the break-in and assault do not warrant my forwarding such a request.'

'Then I hope that one day you have to face up to the consequences of decisions made by people who don't care what happens just so long as the rule book says they're in the clear.'

Upon which Brent left, momentarily hating the detective-inspector almost as much as the men who had intended to attack Susan.

Veronica opened the front door of Mereton Hall. 'Hullo, Jim. Isn't it a lovely day?'

She didn't ask him about the plaster on his neck or the bruise on his cheek. Perhaps, he thought, because of her vague indifference towards anything which didn't directly affect her, she hadn't noticed; perhaps it wasn't considered polite to ask about personal injuries; perhaps she simply didn't give a damn what happened to her daughter's 'policeman' friend. He agreed that it was a lovely day.

'Phillips is hoping it stays fine for the next week because the new bed in the south lawn is just about to come into full flower.'

He managed to show some enthusiasm for the new bed. 'Is Susan in?'

She did not immediately answer, but stared at him, a frown creasing her high forehead. 'I'm rather worried about her. She seems to be upset about something, but when I try to talk to her about it, she won't say a word. Of course, she always has been rather secretive, even when a girl . . . Have you any idea what is the matter?'

'I imagine it's something that's happened because of my work.'

'Oh! . . . Is that also why she's come home?'

'That's right. Is she around?'

'The last time I saw her, she was by the pool.'

'Then I'll go round and see if she's still there.'

He returned to the drive and walked round the west side of the house. This brought him to the stables and a narrow path which ran between them and the walled kitchen garden.

The oval pool was backed by a brick building which contained changing rooms, bathroom, kitchen, and eating area. Susan, wearing the briefest of bikini bottoms and no top, was lying face downwards on a sunbed. When she heard him, she turned her head, identified him, and sat upright.

The sight of her neat, pert breasts triggered an immediate excitement and not for the first time he resentfully wondered why a man's desires should be so easily fired when a woman seemed always to be able to control hers when she wanted to.

'Hullo, sweet,' she said.

'Sweet' was OK, 'love' was common. One needed to know the social dictionary off by heart. He kissed her and cupped her right breast with his hand.

'Not here, not now,' she said, taking hold of his hand and removing it. 'Phillips is working somewhere round about and if he saw us, he'd get all excited and he's too old to risk that. Veronica would never forgive you if he had a heart attack before the village flower show.'

He sat beside her.

'Jim, what's happened?'

'I've discovered that a double bed gets bloody cold when there's only one in it.'

'No, not that; what's happened to you? Have you been in some sort of a fight?'

'Yeah. One of which the Marquis of Queensberry would disapprove.'

'What does that mean?'

'I was feeling chocker last night, so I half hit the whisky. You know how when I do that I wake up in the middle of the night and can't get back to sleep—when I was awake, I heard someone in the house.'

'Oh my God! Did you call the police?'

'That wouldn't have been a very smart move. If I dialled 999, they'd hear me talking and would know I'd sussed them and there was no way the police could reach the house in time to do any good. So I grabbed hold of one of the Indian clubs, put some aerosols on the floor, and waited. When they came into the bedroom, I had the advantage of surprise.'

'How many were there?'

'Four.'

'They were looking for me?'

'It's much more likely they'd broken in on the off-chance, hoping to find something worth nicking,' he said, repeating the possibility which, when the detective-inspector had offered it, he had dismissed with scorn.

She might not have heard him. 'They were going to do all those filthy, disgusting things the man said over the phone.'

'I really don't think—'

'I'd have been raped and worse . . . Oh Christ, I feel sick!'

He reached for her hand to comfort her but, perhaps by chance, she moved it first. 'Susie, I know it's difficult, but don't frighten yourself with thoughts of what might have happened. Remember that it didn't.'

'If I'd been there, they'd have done all those vile things to me.'

'But you weren't there. And in any case, they wouldn't, because I'd have dealt with them, same as I did.' That, of course, was not true. If she'd been at home, he would not have drunk so much whisky and then he would not have been awake to hear them approach the bedroom.

'I . . . I need a drink.' She stood and hurried over to the pool house.

She had not asked him how badly he'd been hurt. Unconcerned about anything but her own fears . . . He cursed himself for his thoughts. It was obvious that he couldn't be badly hurt, so surely it was only natural that her mind should have been primarily occupied with pictures of what could have happened to her . . .

And then his mind once more filled with the fear that was haunting him. There could be no knowing how good was the intelligence of the other side and whether they had managed to identify who she was. If they had, it would be obvious that since she was no longer living in Grangeway, she was possibly back at her parents' home and there would be no difficulty in discovering where that was. A determined assault by several men would overwhelm the defences of alarms and two Rottweilers . . .

It seemed she was not going to pour him a drink. He stood, went into the pool house. He needed one at least as much as she.

A telephone call had established that Hawsley was due back from London on the six o'clock from Cannon Street. Allowing for the drive from Seetonhurst station, he would be arriving at Cockscomb Farm within the next few minutes.

Brent sat behind the wheel of the Escort, parked in the lane, and studied the rear-view mirror. It was with a sense of detached amazement that he realized that the action he was about to take was different only in content and not in form from that which O'Connor had taken; action which he had then viewed with sharp criticism even though he'd supported O'Connor. Those who stressed the absolute need never to be emotionally involved in a case could seldom have been unlucky enough to realize how difficult it could become to do otherwise . . .

The image of a green car—initially too far away to be identified—appeared in the mirror. He watched it approach and, as it passed him, recognized Hawsley at the wheel. He started the engine of the Escort and drove forward.

He parked in the drive and crossed to the garage. Hawsley was stepping out of the Toyota, parked to the left of the BMW, a briefcase in his left hand. As he straightened up and saw Brent, his expression signalled surprise, fear, and finally a determination to bluster. 'You've no right to keep coming here and making a nuisance of yourself.'

'Something's happened that gives me all the right I need. My girlfriend has been receiving threats over the telephone.'

'That's nothing to do with me.'

'You're about to discover that it's got everything to do with you. She was threatened with every filthy, perverted act the caller could think up unless I changed my evidence about finding the drugs on you. Last night four men broke into her house, intending to carry out those threats. Only she wasn't there and I was awake. If she had been there and we'd both been asleep . . .' He suddenly grabbed Hawsley by the coat lapels, balled his right fist, and raised it. Then, after a couple of seconds, during which terror had turned Hawsley's face into a mask, he thrust Hawsley away with such force that he slammed into the side of the car, involuntarily dropping the briefcase. 'If anyone tries that again, I'll do twice to you whatever they do to her. And if you think that that's not possible because she's a woman, you'll be lacking imagination. So you persuade the bastards who hired the heavies to lay off or you're going to be lucky to make hospital.'

Hawsley bolted. He raced round the Toyota, sending something crashing from a shelf, and out through the doorway.

Brent began to leave, set his foot down on something which caused him to lose his balance so that he was only able to prevent himself falling by reaching for the side of the garage. He looked down and saw the briefcase. A chance not to be missed. He picked it up and opened it. Inside were a number of papers, but with one exception these consisted of accounts, statistics, memoranda, graphs, and letters, all pertaining to the Seetonhurst Wine Company. The exception was a bill, made out to Ms Simpson, for £165. He pocketed this and returned the rest of the papers to the briefcase, which he dropped back on the floor.

He got into his car and drove off.

Because it would have been foolhardy to spend the night at Grangeway, he checked in at the section house (so many unmarried officers were now buying their own homes that there were always rooms available). He sat on the bed and looked around himself. Institutional bed, wall cupboard and chest-of-drawers, walls which needed redecorating, faded curtains, and a carpet which had a large burn-hole at its centre. A far cry from the expensively furnished, subtly feminine bedroom at Grangeway . . .

He took the receipt from his coat pocket. Ms Simpson. Mrs or Miss? Why should Hawsley be walking around with a bill for a hundred and sixty-five pounds that was made out to a woman other than his wife? He hoped the answer would make an investigation worthwhile.

CHAPTER 17

Cindy's, in Priory Road, at the back of Knightsbridge, was the kind of shop that a man entered only with reluctance. In the show window were two dresses and three skirts, draped on strangely sculptured wire figures, and several wispy garments; inside were salesladies with carefully cultured accents and a superior lack of enthusiasm for their jobs.

'I suppose,' said a doubtful blonde, 'that she might be able to see you.'

'Perhaps you'd find out?' suggested Brent.

She turned away and went into a small office which led off the shop.

The manageress was a brisk, self-confident woman who wore a dress that shouldn't have suited someone of middle age, but somehow looked right on her. 'You have something to prove that you are a policeman?'

He showed her his warrant card.

'It's just that these days one has to check up on everybody.' She sat behind the desk. 'What exactly is it that you want to know?'

Brent brought out the bill he'd found in Hawsley's briefcase and passed it across. 'Can you identify this customer beyond her name?'

She briefly looked at it. 'I expect the records would say something.'

'Would you check them, then?'

'I'm not certain. Customers expect a large measure of confidentiality from somewhere like this. I think you'll have to give me a good reason for doing so before I agree.'

'I'm on a case and that bill was in the possession of someone who's come to our notice. You'll appreciate that we have to check out everyone, even if any direct connection with the case seems pretty remote. In fact, ninety-nine out of a hundred times, we discover that the person is totally innocent. And when we've established that much, we do what we can to make certain that his or her name doesn't crop up in the case if it comes to court because—as you'll know as well as I do—a lot of mud can stick to the wrong people.'

'I know that only too well . . . All right, I'll see what I can find out.'

She pulled open a drawer in a filing cabinet and looked through some papers. 'The client's full name is Miss Margaret Simpson and she lives at Flat Four C, Winslow Mansions, Prater Street.'

'Can you tell me anything more about her? Is she young, middle-aged, elderly; a frequent customer?'

'I've never served her, but one of my assistants has, several times, and has quite often had a chat with her; some customers can be surprisingly loquacious. Which, of course, is why initially I was reluctant to answer your questions. Miss Simpson is in her middle twenties, quite attractive, but in rather too obvious a manner. Not very much taste— no doubt because of her background—but usually ready to be guided. She buys quite a few clothes here as well as her perfume.'

'It sounds as if she's rich?'

'Lets say one would need a very considerable income to be able to spend as much on clothes and perfume as she does. But the fact is that it is not she who pays the bills.'

'Who does?'

'A gentleman. And if I don't name him, it's not because I'm being very discreet, it's because no one knows his name.'

'Then he doesn't pay by cheque or credit card?'

'Always in cash.'

'Have you ever seen him?'

'Once, very briefly.'

'Can you describe him?'

'Not really. It was quite a long time ago.'

'Could he have been forty-fivish, five feet ten or eleven, mouse-brown hair beginning to thin on top, round face, scar on the right cheek?'

'That could be him, but I'd never swear to it just from the description. As I've said, it was several months ago.'

'Is there anything else you can tell me about Miss Simpson or this man?'

'I don't think so.'

He stood. 'Thanks for your help.'

She looked up at him. 'I've a feeling I may lose a good customer?'

'If you do, don't regret the fact, be damned thankful.'

'That's very cryptic.'

'We have to be even more discreet than you.'

He asked for directions to Prater Street, left. Winslow Mansions was a large Victorian building with patterned brickwork. There was an imposing entrance hall and in this was a desk at which sat a man in uniform. Brent went across. 'I'm visiting Flat Four C.' He turned to cross to the lift.

'Hang on, mate.'

'What's up?'

'She's not expecting you.'

'How would you know?'

'Well, is she?'

'Police.'

The hall porter's expression became one of salacious interest.

The lift took Brent to the fourth floor. Corridors, well carpeted, stretched to the right and left of the small landing and a notice indicated he should go left. He walked along to the door marked 4C and rang the bell, set below a speaker grille. After a while he rang it again, for far longer. There was yet a further wait before a woman's voice, made tinny by the speaker, said: 'What do you want?'

'Miss Simpson?'

'Well?'

'May I have a word with you? My name's Detective-Constable Brent.' There was a sound which could have been a blasphemous expression of surprise. 'If you'd like to see my warrant card, I'll put it up to the spyhole.'

'Wait.'

He waited, becoming more and more impatient as the minutes passed. He remembered the hall porter's certainty that he could not be expected and guessed what was going on inside. He was about to ring the bell again, when he heard her unlock a chain and turn a couple of locks. The door opened.

The manageress of Cindy's had referred to her as 'quite attractive' and had then qualified even this lukewarm praise by obliquely commenting on her lack of taste. Either that description had been coloured by jealousy or all the other customers were potential Miss Universes. She had wavy blonde hair, an oval face with peach-blossom complexion, deep blue eyes, and a curved mouth which added a suggestion of innocent sexuality. Her clothes (surely not approved by Cindy's) were blouse and designer jeans which emphasized a figure it would have been very hard to fault. A slight jumble in her hair, a blouse button undone, and a twist in the jeans, suggested that she had dressed very quickly. 'Sorry to bother you like this,' he said breezily, 'but I've a few questions I'd like to ask.'

'What about?' She was nervous.

'It would be easier if we went somewhere and sat.'

She hesitated, reluctant to agree. He made it clear that he had all the time in the world.

'I suppose you'd better come through,' she finally muttered.

The sitting-room was large, with a picture window that took up most of the outside wall; this was so well insulated that the noise of the traffic was no more than a hum. The furniture was noticeable rather than notable, the carpet was a riot of form and colour, and the framed prints were of work by either a child or a fashionable contemporary artist.

She sat. 'All right, what questions?'

He settled. 'Questions about Ashley Hawsley.'

She was shocked and her face slackened for a couple of seconds as she stared at him wide-eyed. Then she looked away. 'Who's he?'

'Lives near Seetonhurst.'

'Never heard of him.'

'Sure?'

'I said.' She came to her feet and hurried out of the room.

When she returned, she spoke more calmly. 'You've made a mistake.'

'Have I now? Then Ashley Hawsley's an odd sort of a man since he pays all your bills at Cindy's.'

She said wildly: 'Why are you spying on me?'

'Not spying, just making a few inquiries. So tell me about him.'

'Get stuffed.' She reached across to a heavily embossed silver cigarette box, opened this, brought out a cigarette which she lit with a gold lighter.

'Suppose I said I'd like a look around the flat?'

'Where's your warrant?'

'I don't have one. But how can there be any harm?'

'I like my privacy, that's what.'

'There'd be no trouble. I'm broad-minded.'

'What . . . What's that mean?'

'I don't get uptight when I see other people enjoying themselves. For instance, if I found a young man in one of the bedrooms I wouldn't read you a sermon on loyalty, I'd say, Why were you born so lucky?'

'You're talking stupid.'

'Then let's have a little bet on it.'

'It's none of your bloody business who's where.'

'That could be right. I mean, if it doesn't concern me and you've been real helpful, why should I bother Mr Hawsley with the news? Why give the poor man a duodenal?'

She stubbed out the cigarette and left the room.

After a while, he heard the murmur of conversation from the hall. He pictured a man who was trying to get out of the flat as quickly as he could without making that fact obvious. The front door was opened and shut. But it was a further few minutes before she returned to the sitting-room. Now, her hair was in perfect order, no blouse button was undone, and her jeans ran straight. She seemed to have gained a measure of confidence. 'He's a very nice man,' she said, in a throwaway tone.

'Your lucky friend who's just left?'

'Ashley.'

'And you and he are just good friends?'

'Do you have to be so bloody sharp?'

He grinned. 'I'm not sharp, just a bloke who opens his mouth too wide, too often.'

She had not expected mocking self-criticism.

'So now let's establish something. I'm not interested in your lifestyle because that's your business and you're going to fill me in about Hawsley because that's my business.'

'Why?'

'That's called a trade secret.'

She lit another cigarette. 'D'you like champagne?'

'Does a monkey like nuts?'

She stood, went out of the room. When she returned, she carried a tray on which was an ice bucket in which was an unopened bottle and two flutes. She set the tray down on a metal and glass table, filled the glasses, handed him one. Once seated, she drank quickly.

Not her first glass of the day; the explanation of her restored confidence? He drank. 'It's nice. Is this the stuff his firm deals in?'

'Yeah. There's cases in the flat. Sometimes I get fed up with it.'

'The next time you do that, think of me.' He drained his glass and made it obvious that he had.

'You've got legs.'

He crossed to the table, refilled her glass and helped himself. Once more seated, he said: 'You're going to tell me how you came to meet Hawsley.'

At first she spoke slowly and carefully. But after a while— about the middle of the next glassful of champagne—her words came more freely. She'd met Hawsley when he'd still been working in London. There'd been a party at which it was her job to smile sweetly and not shriek if a half-tight Lothario pinched her bottom. Hawsley had chatted to her and since he hadn't tried to grab a quick handful, she'd been happy to spend much of the time with him. He'd driven her back to the small, shoddy flat in Acton which she'd shared with two others and to her surprise he had not suggested a last drink, or something. She'd briefly wondered whether he was a queer who at the party had been using her as camouflage, was the last survivor of that endangered species, the gentleman, or merely nervous?

The next few weeks had shown that he was very nervous— nervous of ever being made to look a fool. He tried to make certain that he never risked suffering an embarrassing rebuff. However, in the end his desires had overcome his sense of caution . . . But what was in it for her with a balding, middle-aged man seeking sex because his wife had almost certainly put up the shutters?

'D'you know, he never talked about her. That's real strange because most of 'em go on and on trying to make it all right with themselves . . .'

Hawsley had vanished from her life. She'd thought—on the rare occasion when she'd bothered to think about him— that he'd given up. But in the middle of one of the toughest times in her life, he'd reappeared. And now, while still middle-aged and balding, he'd been rolling in gold . . .

He'd rented the luxurious flat, given her a hell of a generous allowance, and paid all her bills without question; all he asked in return was that she should love him for himself and not his money, forever be surprised by his vigour, and be faithful. It had been easier to lie to him than to her own body. There were times when she needed the fires which blazed, not those which merely smouldered . . .

'Straight, there've been times when he couldn't manage it.'

'It happens to the best.'

She said archly: 'So how would you know?'

He grinned. 'As a matter of fact, I don't like to boast, but . . .'

'I know. You're the greatest. Never met a man who wasn't. Yet you think there's ten seconds' difference between the lot of you?'

'You're making me very sad.'

'Have another drink.'

He emptied the bottle into her glass.

'There's plenty more in the fridge.'

The kitchen was large and equipped with every type of electrical appliance that was on the market. There was very little food in the double-door refrigerator—suggesting she could seldom be bothered to cook—but there were a dozen bottles of champagne. He brought one out and for the first time studied the label. There was a drawing, in primitive style, of happy peasants—in such surroundings they surely had to be happy?—picking grapes. Underneath, in red lettering, was *Embotellado por Rotga, SA, Sud Perelada*.

Back in the sitting-room, he opened the bottle and topped up her glass before half refilling his own. 'Where d'you reckon all the money comes from?'

'How would I know? He never talks. But I'll tell you one thing. It can't be anything where he takes personal risks.'

An accurate judgement, surely? 'I suppose you've met lots of his friends?'

'You think he'd ever dare risk his wife getting to know about me? Or me meeting someone a lot younger, with the same sort of money?'

'You haven't met anyone?'

'Only that ancient, dumpy dago and that's because he turned up unexpectedly at the hotel. He was enough to give anyone the cringes. When he shook hands, it was like being touched with a slimy sponge.'

'Where was this?'

'Down in Spain, of course.'

'Whereabouts in Spain?'

'I don't know. Can't remember names. But it was close to where they make all the wine his firm imports.'

'So what were you doing down there?'

'Ashley always takes me. Before we went the first time, I got real excited—a posh hotel, sun, sand, sea, a luxury yacht, and Paul Newmans everywhere . . . Didn't turn out like that, did it? When he went off to do some work, I had to stay in the hotel suite because he was scared I'd take a quick tumble with one of the waiters.'

'What was this Spaniard's name?'

'Joan.' She giggled. 'I thought he must be a trans. But it seems like that really is a man's name in the lingo they talk.'

'So what was his surname?'

'I don't know. What's it bloody matter?'

'What did this Spaniard do?'

'Jeeze, you must get paid for asking questions.' She drank deeply, lit another cigarette.

'Did he work for the wine company?'

'Yeah.'

'If he turned up unexpectedly, what was the problem?'

'Ashley kicked me off into the bedroom and made me shut the door.'

'Which annoyed you so much you listened at the keyhole.'

She giggled again.

'What did you hear?'

'Can't you think of something more interesting to talk about?'

'What were they talking about?'

She swore, pouted, drank, finally answered. 'I couldn't hear properly, but it was to do with money—Ashley moved nearer to the door and I could hear him saying he ought to have more.'

'More than what?'

'I don't know. He moved away again.'

'So what happened?'

'The dago left and Ashley was in a filthy temper. But the next day he went out and when he came back he was all smiles and—'

'What?'

'Goddamnit, who's interested?'

'I am.'

'He was all smiles because his briefcase was stuffed full of dollars.'

'How d'you know that?'

'Had a look, didn't I, when he was in the john . . . Come on, give me another glass and let's do some drinking.'

'Sorry, but I have to move on; late already.' He stood.

She stared up at him. 'What's the rush? Scared?' she asked angrily, her words slightly slurred.

CHAPTER 18

Before entering the canteen for supper, Brent checked the noticeboard to the right of the doorway. Pinned on to it, on two pieces of paper, in different handwriting, were messages for him. Detective-Sergeant O'Connor wanted him to ring immediately. Detective-Inspector Fawcus said he was to report to his office at nine o'clock the following morning.

He went into the canteen, picked up a tray, pushed it along the rails as he chose a salad, sausages and baked beans, and apple pie. The woman at the till said he was looking a bit peaky and he needed a holiday. He asked her to go with him to Brighton for the coming weekend and all thirteen stone wobbled as she laughed.

He ate quickly at a table on his own, conscious of the fact that if he had joined any of the other diners he would have caused embarrassment; a suspended detective was not the most welcome of companions.

He left the canteen, searched his pockets for change, dialled O'Connor's number on the telephone that was six feet from the doorway. 'Pam, I'm just back and there's a note that Hugh wants a word.'

'Hold on a moment.'

She must have heard about the fight in Grangeway on the previous Friday night, yet she had not asked him how he now was, although she was normally someone who was concerned about other people. Involvement in a crime changed people in ways that could never be foreseen.

'What's the old man want?' demanded O'Connor, without any initial greeting. 'He's been on to me twice during the day, asking where you'd got to. I told him, I didn't know, but I don't reckon he believed me. What's he after?'

'I haven't spoken to him and all I know is that there's a note telling me to report to him at nine tomorrow.'

'You're not . . . not intending to tell him what happened?'

'You imagine I would be?'

'It's just that . . . He sounded as if it were really urgent and I thought . . . I'm sorry, Jim, but everything's so bloody. I mean, if they do decide to hold an internal hearing and things should go wrong . . .'

'They can't, provided each of us stays cool, calm and collected; and doesn't start thinking the other's blowing the gaff.'

'I really know you'd never let me down, but it's . . . You've got to understand . . .'

Brent listened to the halting apologies, knowing that whatever happened now their friendship could never survive unaltered.

The DI normally dressed carefully, but he was too tired and stressed to look smart. 'I gave you credit for some intelligence, but what do you do? You return to Cockscomb Farm and assault Mr Hawsley.'

'No, sir,' said Brent, as he stood in front of the desk.

'He says you grabbed him by the coat, bunched your fist, and threatened to beat him up if anyone went after your girlfriend.'

'I spoke to him in the garage. I did not touch his coat, I

did not bunch my fist, and I did not threaten him. I merely asked him to do what he could to make certain that Miss Radford is not drawn any further into the affair.'

'You expect me to believe that?'

'Lacking any proof to the contrary, yes, I do. If possible, most detective-inspectors believe their own DCs.'

'If possible. That just about lines it up.'

'Is Mrs Hawsley again falsely claiming to have been present?'

'No.'

'Then it's Mr Hawsley's word against mine. That leaves you free to believe me—should you by any chance wish to.'

'You're very insolent.'

'All I'm trying to do is to protect Miss Radford.'

'And you think you can best do that by threatening assault? Have you still not learned?'

'I have learned one thing. Try to protect a potential victim by appealing to the law and you're wasting your breath.'

Fawcus said with angry weariness: 'Bring me proof that the men who broke into the house did so because Hawsley is engaged in the drug trade and I will forward the recommendation to the Chief Superintendent that Miss Radford is given immediate protection round the clock.'

'How can I prove anything when you've suspended me?'

Fawcus slammed his fist down on the desk. 'Did your suspension stop you returning to Cockscomb Farm and threatening Hawsley? When it comes to your career, you're your own worst enemy.'

'Because I don't keep one eye on the rule book all the time?'

'Because you refuse to understand that there is a good reason for every rule; that those who help in the administration of the law must be seen to live by it; that it's better a guilty man goes free than that he is convicted on false evidence.'

'Better for his next victim?'

'Better for justice.'

'One hopes the victim appreciates that.'

'All right, that's all I have to say for the moment. Before you leave the building, you'll deliver to me a full report on the incident concerning Mr Hawsley.'

Mereton Hall was looking attractive in the late afternoon sunshine. Although man-made, it was at one with the land and the sky.

Mrs Weston opened the front door. 'Miss Susan's out,' she said, her speech impediment more obvious than usual.

'D'you know when she'll be back?' Brent asked.

'I can't rightly say.'

'Is Mrs Radford in?'

'She's watching the telly.'

He went through to the smaller sitting-room and began to speak to Veronica. ''Afternoon. Do you know when Susan—'

'Just a minute,' she said, without taking her eyes off the screen.

He sat and watched the horses round the turn and come into the straight. To his surprise, as two drew clear of the bunch she excitedly called on one of them to go still faster. It was the first time he had seen any signs of emotion in her.

One horse just pipped the other at the post.

He said: 'Have you any idea when Susan will be back?'

'There's an objection! Why? He ran straight. It's quite ridiculous.'

She ignored him until the commentator said that the objection had been overruled. Number seven was confirmed the winner, at three to one. 'I had five pounds on him!' she said triumphantly.

Other people never ceased to astonish him. Susan was in danger and his arrival might mean he had information which could increase or lessen such danger, yet all that immediately concerned her mother was the fact that she had won fifteen pounds. Fifteen pounds to her would be like fifteen pence to him. 'Do you know when Susan will be back?' he asked for the third time.

'I'm afraid I don't.'

'She was out to lunch?'

'I'm not certain.'

Veronica might be vague, but she could hardly be that vague. It was her well-bred way of telling him that he did not have the right to ask what Susan was doing. 'D'you mind if I wait around to see if she'll be back soon?'

'Certainly. You will have some tea?'

The more they disliked you, the politer they became; politeness was a weapon both of offence and defence.

Susan arrived home an hour later, by which time Veronica and he were watching a trite quiz programme on the television because that was much easier than talking to each other. He stood as she entered the room and there was a tight feeling inside him because she was so vitally attractive.

'Hullo, Jim. How are things?'

She might have been greeting a casual friend, but then he had not expected her to show him affection in front of her mother. 'Not so bad, except for the grub. In my book, the cook should be prosecuted under the trade description acts.'

'Poor man . . . I'm all hot and sticky and feel like a swim. Join me?'

'It sounds a good idea.'

'Then go on down and I'll meet you there. You'll find some trunks somewhere in the pool house.'

They left together and parted in the hall. He went out by the front door and round to the pool. Once changed, he sat on the side, his feet dangling in the heated water. When he heard her approach, he turned. She was wearing a one-piece costume he had not seen before that was cut on lines which years before would have made even a grandfather leer. 'My God, that gives a man ideas!'

'Since when did your imagination require a trigger?'

He'd been about to suggest that they retire into the pool house and, away from the prying eyes of the gardener, discover just how little his imagination did need stimulating. But the tone with which she'd spoken had made it clear that any such suggestion would be rebuffed. Uninhibited in Grangeway, it seemed that in her parents' home she was virtuously discreet.

'Come on in,' she offered. 'Race you two lengths, giving me five yards' start.'

'Like hell! We both start from scratch.' She had been taught at school and had a stylish crawl, he had taught himself and although his strokes were powerful, they were also wasteful.

She dived suddenly, catching him unawares, and had gained the five yards' lead before he hit the water. The finish was very close and each of them was able to claim to have won. They left the pool to stretch out on towels and dry in the sun.

'What have you been doing with yourself?' she asked.

'What I can to make certain you're completely safe. I began by getting hold of a certain gentleman and advising him that if anything happens to you, I'll take him apart, inch by nasty inch.'

'You really did?' She turned her head to look directly at him. 'Yes. You've that teeth-in-the-flesh look. A very nasty experience for him. What did he do?'

'Squeaked and ran.'

'I wish I'd been there to see it. A touch of the cave suits a man. Anything else?'

'I had a chat and sank a few bottles of bubbly with a very attractive prosey.'

'Is she what I think she is?'

'In this case, a twenty-five-year-old who was on the game

but who's found a man rich enough to keep her in luxury, but stupid enough not to bribe the hall porter to tell him who she's entertaining when it's not him.'

'Did you give her hell as well?'

He so often felt at a disadvantage in her company. For him, certain relationships were too important to be mocked, but she seemed to believe that nothing was sacrosanct. 'You think I'd ever threaten a woman?'

'Some like that. Was she able to help you?'

'I'm not certain.'

'That hardly sounds like you.'

'I don't know whether I'm seeing possibilities that weren't really there.'

'Even less like you.'

'On the face of things, she couldn't tell me anything useful. But she may have let something important slip without realizing it. She and the man I'm interested in have been several times down to Spain where he carried out business with the Spanish company with whom his English company deals. Why does he go down there?'

'Tell me.'

'It could be for a very ordinary reason until you know that one day an employee of the Spanish company unexpectedly came to the hotel. Obviously, the reason for the meeting was potentially dangerous to them because the woman was ordered into the bedroom, with the door firmly shut. Naturally, she listened through the keyhole to as much as she could. The Englishman demanded more money. The next day his briefcase was full of dollar notes.'

'The inference being that that money was a bribe?'

'It almost certainly was, but a bribe to do, or not to do, what? Perhaps to keep his mouth shut?'

'About what?'

'The obvious answer has to be that he'd discovered the Spaniard was screwing someone.'

'You mean financially and not the more amusing variety?'

He turned over, sat up, and linked his arms about his raised legs. 'The case is about drugs, but so far we've been unable to prove a thing. The Englishman's company imports wine from Spain and, as far as anyone knows, is perfectly legitimate. He lives in a far from grand house, runs a company car, and his wife has a small BMW. No signs that he's living beyond his salary. That is, until one knows that he rents a very expensive flat in London and stocks it with a very smart number who's given spending money by the bucketful and has all her bills paid.

'Spain's become a hot distribution centre for drugs from South America, largely because of her past colonial connections. Up in Galicia, the drug-runners are using boats to land cargoes from ships that can better sixty knots and outrun anything the government has. So it would make a lot of sense for a Spanish company to supply drugs to an English company under the guise of normal trading. The Englishman isn't the type to get his hands dirty, so since he's an accountant, his job may be to make certain from the figures that no one's screwing his bosses. A bribe offered and accepted would suggest he's discovered evidence of such a screwing, but is prepared to keep quiet about this.' He became silent.

'And?'

'That's it.'

'Why isn't someone doing something?'

'Because most of what I've said is supposition and not hard fact.'

'Search the English company's place and uncover the facts.'

'That's impossible without a search warrant, which won't be granted without sufficient proof. And since all the time there's a detective-inspector who takes the rule book to bed with him, sufficient proof means a cast-iron case.'

'You said that the accountant's got this woman up in London and is spending a fortune on her. Isn't that proof enough he's up to something?'

'Only that he's spending more than he's earning; until you've been through all his finances, you can't be certain that he hasn't the private means to supply the difference. And until you can pin a criminal probability on him, you can't get permission to investigate his finances.'

'That's stupid.'

'And dangerous, because until they're uncovered . . .'

'I'm in danger?' She reached out and gripped his hand. Once again, fear had stripped away her sophisticated certainty. 'You've got to persuade the Detective-Inspector to do something.'

'He won't do a bloody thing until there's proof.'

'But you said there can't be any until something's done.'

'That's right.'

'Then . . . then what?'

'If I can persuade Maggie to describe the Spaniard sufficiently well for me to identify him, I could go down to Spain and question him. Maybe he'll supply some proof.'

'If Maggie's the woman in London, why haven't you already gone back and got her to do that?'

'One reason is that a woman like her talks for money. And right now my bank balance wouldn't persuade a five-year-old.'

'How much do you want?'

He would never have asked her directly for the money because that, however illogically, would have made him feel that he was poncing. 'I'd like to have a thousand. To begin with, I wouldn't need anything like that because she won't realize the value of her information, but the extra would get me down to Spain.'

'I'll give you a cheque and you can cash it tomorrow as soon as the banks open.'

'I'll pay you back as soon as I can.'

She didn't bother to try to find the words that might have eased his embarrassment at having to accept her money.

CHAPTER 19

The hall porter at Winslow Mansions grinned salaciously. 'More pressing business?'

'That's right,' Brent answered.

'Some blokes have all the luck.'

He took the lift up to the fourth floor and Flat 4C, rang the bell. There was only a short wait before Maggie opened the door. She was wearing a silk negligee over a nightdress. 'What d'you want now?' Her expression was strained and her tone harshly antagonistic, suggesting a pounding headache.

'I've one or two more questions.'

'Suppose I don't want to answer 'em?'

'You're too sensible to be like that.'

She hesitated, then turned and crossed the hall to the sitting-room. He shut the front door, followed her. She had settled on the settee, legs tucked under her.

'Well, what questions?' She reached for a cigarette.

'D'you remember telling me about the Spaniard called Joan whom you met in Spain?'

'And if I do?' She shifted and as she did so the negligee gaped to show that the nightdress was made of a very fine, semi-transparent material. She made no effort to rearrange the negligee.

'Did you learn what sort of a position he had in the Spanish firm?'

'I didn't learn anything. I said, I was kicked into the bedroom. All I know is, his hand felt like something beginning to rot.'

'His surname wasn't mentioned?'

'That's right, it wasn't.'

'Try and describe him.'

'Why the hell should I?' She moved her legs and the negligee gaped further. She said scornfully: 'So how far up can you see?'

He shrugged his shoulders.

'What's the matter? You don't like admitting you get all excited looking up the legs of a slag? Christ, men are hypocrites! Are you married?'

'No.'

'But you've got a woman and she's not a slag like me?'

'D'you give yourself a thrill every time you use that word?' She swore.

'Was Joan tall, medium, or short; thin or fat; black hair, brown hair, becoming bald?'

'I've forgotten.'

'Then start remembering.'

'You think that because I'm a slag, I'm stupid? Ashley's into something which pays real money. You're on to Ashley because you reckon that that something is nasty. But you can't do anything and you think that maybe that dago in Spain will help you . . . But if you talk to him, maybe what he says means you can nick Ashley. Where would that leave me? Bleeding cold, that's where. So I'd have to be real thick to tell you anything more.'

'We'll land him, whether you do or don't.'

'Yeah? If it was that way, you wouldn't be here now.'

'All I'm looking for is a short cut. So why not help yourself to a future with some security?'

'How much security?'

'Two centuries.'

She laughed jeeringly. 'You think I'll rush for a couple of hundred? I wouldn't for a couple of thousand. They chose a right country boy when they picked you!'

He belatedly realized that he had been very naïve to believe money held the same proportional value for her as it did for him. 'He's into drugs,' he said harshly.

'So?'

'Don't you realize what that means?'

'He's richer than I thought so I can keep on shopping.'

'D'you know what the drug trade means in terms of broken lives?'

'What are you asking me—have I seen people get hooked? Don't you know a bloody thing about life? I've seen more people killing themselves on dope than you've seen summers.'

'Then here's a chance for you to help others escape that.'

'You're asking me to be a Girl Guide? Sod 'em.'

He wondered if there was any point in continuing the questioning and decided there was not. Yesterday she had been half drunk and frightened and therefore carelessly prepared to talk; today she was neither. He stood.

'You're leaving so soon?' she asked mockingly. 'Don't you want to know what the dago looks like, then?'

'Yes.'

'Then why don't you ask nicely and I'll describe him right down to the ugly big mole on his neck. And if I really tried, maybe I'd remember that I did hear what his surname was.' She moved her legs out from under her and stood. She shed the negligee. More slowly, she reached down to the hem of the nightdress and lifted it up and over her head. Her body was every bit as shapely as he had imagined it.

She came forward, stopped when immediately in front of him. She took hold of his right hand and held it to herself. She said in a husky whisper: 'So now prove that you're the best.'

Desire made a pulse in his neck hammer, tightened his stomach, and swept his mind. But then as she pressed against him, he caught the scent that she was wearing and it reminded him of Susan's favourite.

He jerked himself free, with sufficient force to send her staggering sideways. He crossed to the doorway, went through the hall and out to the passage. As he walked towards the lift, he thought that, incredibly, there'd been a moment in the sitting-room when he'd become so self-deluded that he'd believed it was an overwhelming desire

for him that motivated her; all too clearly, he could now see
that her motivation had been hatred and that the only desire
she had experienced had been to prove that he could, with
contemptuous ease, be degraded into having sex with a
woman he labelled slag.

It was odd that the idea had not come to him before. Angrily
subduing any thought that perhaps it had come to him now
because of what had happened—to imagine that a desire
for Susan could be fuelled by the sight of a naked Maggie
was a blasphemy—he assured himself it was because he'd
had of necessity been giving more thought to business than
to pleasure. He dialled the number, watched the assistant
in the travel agent's as he waited.

'Yes?' said Mrs Weston, who could never be persuaded
to answer the telephone formally.

'It's Jim Brent. Is Miss Susan in?' He always found it
absurd to say 'Miss Susan'. But Veronica was not vague
when it came to dealing with 'them' and insisted on anti-
quated formalities.

'I think she's here. Hang on.'

As he waited, he wondered whether the assistant behind
the counter, who was leafing through a brochure of package
holidays, sold to herself the same daydreams that she sold
to others . . .

'Yes, Jim?'

'How are you, darling?'

'Fine.'

'Are you sure? You sound odd.'

'I was outside and had to hurry. I'm a bit breathless,
that's all.'

'Look, I've had a great idea. Come to Spain with me. I've
been given the name of a first-class hotel and it wouldn't be
anything like you've always feared; it's right on the beach,
quite a distance from anywhere else, there's no madding
crowd, and the food isn't chips-with-everything.'

'It sounds fun, but I'm sorry . . .'

'It'll get you away from the slightest chance of any trouble.'

'There isn't any now.'

He was perplexed by what she'd said. 'Why not?'

'Chris had a word with the Chief Constable and now we're under special police watch. A patrol car turns up at odd hours and has a look around to see that all's quiet. Of course, Veronica's complaining because at night the car wakes her since she's such a light sleeper.'

'It's great news about the police.' He hoped he sounded enthusiastic and not resentful. His request to the Detective Chief Superintendent and to Fawcus for police protection for Susan had been refused on the grounds that there was not sufficient proof of danger to warrant such an expense in time, money, and manpower. Yet Radford had only to have a private word with the Chief Constable for all those considerations to be ignored. 'But that doesn't stop you having fun in the sun.'

'I'd love to, Jim, but a couple of ancient relatives are coming for a stay and I've promised Veronica I'll help cope with them.'

'Get hold of that cousin of Mrs Weston who'll always give a hand when there's extra work. I really want you to come . . .'

'And I would if I could, but I just can't.'

When the call was over, he said to the nearer assistant: 'It's just the one ticket after all.'

CHAPTER 20

He took the shuttle from Barcelona airport to Sants station, where he had to queue for so long to buy a ticket that he only just managed to catch the Catala Talgo to Figueres.

There, a taxi drove him through flat, well-farmed countryside, whose backdrop was the Pyrenees, to the Bahia Azul.
Despite accepting package holidaymakers, the hotel still
offered a service to the independent traveller and the receptionist smiled and wished him a happy stay.

The bedroom, which had an en-suite bathroom, was
large and it overlooked the beach. He walked on to the
balcony, edged with elaborate wrought-iron railings,
and stared down at a young woman who was walking
out of the sea and on to the beach. She was topless
and very nearly bottomless. He cursed Susan's ancient
relations before going down to the desk and arranging
with the concierge to hire a car and to secure the services
of an interpreter.

Carlos Blanco, roughly Brent's age, spoke idiosyncratic
English with a generous American accent. 'I spend four
years in Chicago learning the hotel business so I speak
good.' Short and stockily built, his face was sharply featured
in typical Catalan style. 'Now you say to me, señor, where
you wish to go and what you wish to do.'

'Do you know the Rotga Winery?' Brent answered, hoping
Blanco would prove to be not quite so full of himself as
initial acquaintance suggested.

'The Rotga Winery . . .' Blanco thought as he rubbed his
chin, fashionably shaded by stubble. He let go of his chin
and snapped his fingers. 'But of course! How could I not
know instantly? It is near my Uncle Pedro's finca. You wish
to visit there and see how wine is made? It is not the right
season . . .'

'I want to try and contact an employee.'

'Then let us travel.'

Whatever happened, Brent thought as they left the hotel
and walked towards the car park, he had to conceal the fact
that he was a policeman. Carrying on an inquiry without
the knowledge and consent of the Spanish police was a

procedural sin of such proportions that even the DI would be astonished by his recklessness . . . He unlocked the Ford Fiesta which had earlier been delivered by a hire company, settled behind the wheel, and started the engine. 'Which way do we go when we leave here?'

A thirty-five minutes' journey through countryside that was first flat and then rolling brought them to the winery. A three-storey, modern building fronted several much older and barn-like ones. The surrounding fields were all down to vines and these were pruned to the boles each winter so that the summer growth was not high enough to need support.

They entered the office block through an imposing doorway with marble columns and inside was a large reception area, on the far wall of which hung a portrait in oils of the founder of the firm. The reception desk was set below this and the expression on the severe face suggested the founder had probably been regretting the fact that he would not always personally be able to make certain that the staff were giving full value in return for their wages.

The receptionist was young, attractive, and smartly dressed. Blanco, now very full of machismo, spoke to her at unnecessary length. She was unimpressed, but interested in Brent. Blanco said: 'You tell me what you want and she will help because of me.'

'Will you explain that I have a friend who was out here last summer and a man who works for this company was very kind to him. My friend intended to send a small present by way of thanks, but when he returned home he found he'd lost the bit of paper on which he'd written down the name and address. He heard I was coming out here and asked me if I'd try and find them out for him. I thought that the only thing to do was to come here and describe the man and hope someone could identify him from that description. I know it all sounds a bit crazy . . .' Brent smiled at the receptionist.

Blanco translated. The receptionist picked up the receiver of the nearer telephone and spoke into it.

'She is trying,' said Blanco. 'She thinks it is best if at the beginning you speak with the foreman.'

It seemed she had accepted his explanation, thought Brent; Blanco probably had not, since he looked as if he were trying to work out what was really going on and whether there was some way in which he could cut himself into it.

The receptionist replaced the receiver, spoke to Blanco. Blanco said in English: 'The foreman will arrive and speak.'

There was a brief wait, then a short, stocky man with a full beard, wearing a stained leather apron over rough serge clothes, came through one of the four doorways. Surprisingly, instead of the deep voice which might have been expected from someone of his build and appearance, his voice was almost squeaky.

Blanco translated. 'He will do what he can.'

'Will you thank him for his help?'

'When we find he knows something,' was the somewhat graceless reply.

'Explain that the man who helped my friend is probably in his late fifties or early sixties, not very tall, rather over-weight and, for what it's worth, has a very flabby handshake; there's a noticeable mole on his neck; and his Christian name is Joan.'

As soon as Blanco had passed on this information it was clear that his words had had considerable effect. The foreman talked loudly to the receptionist as she talked excitedly to him, and from time to time they both addressed Blanco at the same moment. It took some little while for them to calm sufficiently for him to understand what they were saying. 'They think that perhaps you speak of Joan Capllonch.'

'Why should that get them buzzing like a hive of disturbed hornets?'

'Because he is disappeared.'

CHAPTER 21

The Guardía Civil barracks were built along traditional lines. A high wall surrounded the complex and this was broken by only one gateway; immediately inside was a large administrative block, in the centre of which was an archway which gave access to the square beyond; around the square were the buildings in which the guards and their families lived—it was the policy of the corps that no member ever served in his home province.

Half way along the arched throughway, on the left-hand side, was the front office. A cabo, with the dark olive complexion that placed him as having come from the south, sat behind a desk and dealt with inquiries from the public—a far from onerous task since few Spaniards ever voluntarily had anything to do with the guardía. He listened to Blanco, then said that he'd have to go and speak to someone. He stood and crossed the small room to go through a doorway. When he returned, he was accompanied by a sargento.

The sergento, whose manner was latently aggressive, studied Brent as he listened to Blanco. Blanco, whose manner had become relatively subdued, said: 'He tells me he knows nothing.'

'He must have some idea of what happened?'

The sargento shrugged his shoulders and it seemed for a while that that was to be his only answer; then, after this tight-lipped silence, he suddenly spoke at considerable length.

Blanco said: 'Capllonch lives in Rueda with his wife and one of his sons who works in the cork forests. He went out one evening with friends and did not come back. His car also is disappeared. It was a Mercedes. It is a great pity for a Mercedes to disappear.' It seemed that he found the loss of the car more distressing than the loss of the man.

'Can't these friends say what's happened to him?'

'No one knows who they are because they are not of the region. Perhaps they come from Madrid.' In Catalonia, the font of all problems was Madrid.

'And his wife can't suggest who they might be?'

'She says she has not seen them ever until this time.'

'Does he often go out with strangers?'

Blanco put the question to the sargento, who answered curtly. 'He says, why do you ask so many questions?'

'I'm just curious. When I see my friend in England again, I'd like to be able to tell him all I can.'

'The sargento says you know everything.'

To continue would be to excite more suspicion than he had already aroused. Brent passed on the thanks of his friend and then said goodbye.

As Brent sat out on the balcony of his hotel room, growing darkness first scrambled the horizon and then eliminated it and sea and sky merged. For the umpteenth time he asked himself whether it was a coincidence that Capllonch had disappeared, for the umpteenth time he answered that on the few facts available, it was impossible to give a worthwhile answer.

And yet . . . And yet the missing Capllonch was almost certainly the man whom Margaret Simpson had seen in the hotel room who had handed Hawsley a fortune in dollars—money which surely had to have come from an illegal operation. And yet Capllonch owned a Mercedes and that was a very expensive car for a man who worked in the bottling department . . .

Experience and an inside knowledge of how much of the drug trade worked painted a scenario into which the few known facts fitted snugly. The Rotga Winery was a legitimate business engaged in a legitimate trade; it was also the front for drug-trafficking. In its first identity it engaged in a regular trade with Britain, shipping wine and spirits; in the second it used that regular trade to transport drugs, hidden in any one of a dozen possible ways. Capllonch had worked for both the legitimate and the illegitimate side of the business.

The extra money made from his part in the drug trade had introduced Capllonch to a standard of life that had once been beyond even his wildest dreams. But greed fed on dreams and dreams fed on greed. When he calculated the fantastic profits made by those for whom he worked, his extra money began to seem like very small beer and he wanted more. To want was to work out how to get. He had started stealing small quantities of drugs, confident that these modest thefts could never be uncovered.

Hawsley was an accountant whose work could be split into three distinct categories; he supervised the financial affairs of the legitimate business of the Seetonhurst Wine Company; he checked all the figures relating to their criminal business, making certain that no one was ripping off the bosses; he supervised the laundering of the illegal profits. It was in his second capacity that he had uncovered evidence of the theft at the winery and then the identity of the thief.

Just as greed had fuelled the dreams of Capllonch, so it had now fuelled those of Hawsley. If he reported what he'd discovered to his bosses, Capllonch would be murdered and the most he could expect would be a verbal pat on the back; but if he blackmailed Capllonch into taking him into partnership, he could make a fortune and do all the things that the really rich did, such as setting up a beautiful and passionate woman in a luxury flat. And who could ever discover what was going on when the person in charge of detection was himself? Who guards the guards themselves? . . . One answer to that question was that the bosses would, if they learned that Capllonch was selling drugs on his own account.

That Hawsley was still alive must mean that his partnership with Capllonch had not come to light. Perhaps the
bosses had been too certain that Capllonch had been working on his own; perhaps they'd been too eager to have him
eliminated to arrange to have him interrogated before he
was murdered; perhaps they'd arranged, but his interroga-
tors had been ham-fisted and had killed him before he'd
had time to tell them anything.

So there was the scenario. Yet it was built up on few facts
and much surmise. Go to the Spanish police and ask them to
find out how much of the surmise was fact and they would
be completely justified in treating him as an interfering fool
who'd broken all the rules and their only action would be to
lodge the strongest of protests with the British authorities . . .
He experienced bitter frustration. Susan remained at risk.
She believed she was out of danger because the police were
giving her individual protection, but to a good hit squad, a
patrol car was at most a minor irritant . . . It was easy to
picture the hit squad, waiting until the police car had driven
off and, knowing it would not return for some time, moving
forward. The two Rottweilers would easily be drugged. A
specialist would immobilize the alarms. Once in the house,
they would search the bedrooms, find her . . .

He'd told himself that there was nothing more he could
do. That was wrong. Provided only that he was prepared
to stick his neck out even further—and to ensure Susan's
safety, he'd risk anything—there was something. He could
discover whether Capllonch owned a Mercedes because he
was a man who saw a car as the ultimate status symbol and
was prepared to scrimp in every other part of his life in
order to obtain one, or whether this was just the most visible
indication that his lifestyle could never be sustained by his
wages.

Brent spoke to the concierge at the hotel and explained that
he needed another interpreter because Blanco had said that

he was too busy to do any more work; the concierge accepted the lie without any hesitation and promised that there would be not the slightest difficulty in finding someone else. Brent was glad. Blanco had already become too curious; the proposed visit would have raised that curiosity to fever pitch.

Aznar could hardly have been of a more different character. Approaching middle age, he was quiet almost to the point of diffidence. He said that the drive to Rueda would take almost an hour, since it was up in the foothills of the Pyrenees, and appeared totally uninterested in the reason why Brent should wish to meet a family about whom he knew nothing.

In the event, the drive took them just over the hour because the road through the cork forests was narrow and winding, the majority of the many hairpin bends were unfenced, and Brent was using all the extra care of someone who had done very little Continental driving and was not happy at being on the 'wrong' side of the road.

Rueda was perched on and about the crest of a hill and its narrow cobbled streets, totally unsuited to modern traffic, were sometimes so steep that they had had to be stepped. The houses, all small, were built of stone and they huddled together for protection in the winters, which could be bitter since they were not far below the five hundred metre level.

Aznar went into a shop—there was no show window and nothing on the outside to suggest it was a shop; one had to push through a bead curtain to discover that it was—and asked where the Capllonch family lived. The two customers stared at him with distrust and the woman behind the rough wooden counter took so long to answer that it had begun to seem that she would not.

'I fear that they are difficult people,' Aznar said, as they returned to the road. 'She did not wish even to tell me where the family lives. These villages are isolated and the people who live in them do not like strangers.'

'I don't suppose they see many up here?'

'There is no reason to come.'

They turned into a street so steep it had been stepped. This ended in a relatively flat area around which were five houses in a rough semi-circle. Outside one, a donkey with a pannier on either side was tethered to a large iron ring.

'I believe it is here.' Aznar made for the house immediately to their right, the front door of which was reached by going down three steps. Conforming to tradition, he pushed through the bead curtain, went inside, and called out.

They were in a sitting-room. The three-piece suite was new and covered in first quality leather, there was a large and very ornately inlaid sideboard and a glass-fronted cabinet filled with Lladro figures, the carpet would not have disgraced a rich man's castle, the television was huge, and by its side was an elaborate stacked deck music centre with free-standing speakers a metre high.

A woman, her coarse, round face deeply lined by age, past hardships and present sorrow, wearing a shapeless black frock, entered through the far doorway. She stared at them, but offered no greeting.

Aznar spoke. She shook her head. He spoke again and at greater length and she abruptly turned and went back the way she had come. Aznar said: 'It is very difficult. You must please understand, the people who live in these villages are not like other Catalans . . .' He came to a stop.

'We've got people just as suspicious of foreigners.' Brent moved across the room to read the make of the television. Sony. The only people he knew back home who had a TV of that size and expense were Susan's parents. Leather furniture was surely as much a luxury in Spain as it was almost everywhere else? The carpet must have cost a fortune. The sideboard and display cabinet were new . . .

Capllonch's wife—or widow—returned and with her was a man whose surly face so closely resembled hers that he was unmistakably her son. He spoke roughly, gesticulating angrily as he did so.

Aznar said to Brent, 'He demands to know who you are and why you are asking questions.'

'Explain, will you, and say that I wondered if the family had heard anything about his father who was so kind to my friend.'

As he listened to Aznar, the son stared fixedly at Brent, his expression glowering. Then he turned on his heel and stamped out.

'He refuses to speak,' said Aznar, stating the obvious. 'I will ask the mother again.'

She shook her head.

'I am sorry, señor, but I believe we will learn nothing. I have a strange feeling. It is almost as if . . .' He stopped, hesitated, resumed. 'As if they are scared to speak. But that, of course, is impossible. Why should they be frightened? I am mistaking the stupid suspicion of everyone who is not from their own village.'

Brent wondered if Aznar were talking nonsense? He hadn't understood a word either mother or son had spoken, yet there had seemed to him to be an undercurrent which might well have been fear.

When they left, the woman merely stared at them with the same sullen dislike and did not return their goodbyes. The Fiesta was parked on the side of the only road leading into the village. Brent unlocked the doors, settled behind the wheel, started the engine, made a clumsy three-point turn because the road was narrow and he was reluctant to get too close to the unfenced edge. Before driving off, he checked in the rear-view mirror and had a last glimpse of Rueda, which seemed to glower even in the sharp sunshine; he noticed that a Land-Cruiser was leaving the village and momentarily wondered who had been so stupid as to take a vehicle that size among the narrow, twisting streets.

He drove slowly, taking the hairpin bends at speeds that would have evoked the contempt of any young Spanish driver and he was not, therefore, surprised to see the Land-Cruiser appear in the rear-view mirror. What did vaguely surprise him, however, was that the other vehicle did not overtake on what was a relatively safe stretch of road, but slowed to match his speed.

They rounded a left-hand hairpin to face another, at least as sharp, five hundred metres below. The Land-Cruiser closed but still did not try to pass. He changed down to second for the corner. Here, the land dropped away sharply, but the road remained unfenced.

Once round the corner, the Land-Cruiser drew out. Since it was less than two hundred metres to the next corner, this was, he thought, a typical piece of dangerous driving; perhaps the driver had decided that machismo demanded he get past this mimsing tourist, regardless of conditions. He braked, to give the other more room and time for the stupid manœuvre. The Land-Cruiser drew abreast, but instead of accelerating past, it closed.

His immediate reaction was that the driver had to be drunk. Then, as he instinctively looked sideways to gauge relative speeds and distances, he caught sight of the passenger's face and he abruptly realized that this was not a case of drunkenness.

He had always had fast reactions and police work had taught him not to let emotion affect those reactions; surprise, shock, fear, could have slowed him down, but did not. He braked fiercely and the car began to slide, a movement he killed with opposite lock. Aznar, unprepared, was thrown sideways and his seat-belt automatically tightened; he made a sound that was half exclamation, half cry.

The Land-Cruiser braked equally fiercely and smoke came off the heavy duty tyres as it swerved into the path of the Ford. Brent floored the accelerator as he steered to his right, trying to make the closing gap. Tyres scrabbled the edge of the road, there was light contact of metal to metal which jolted them, then they were through.

He kept the accelerator hard down, hoping to break clear, but the Land-Cruiser was faster, due to a highly turbocharged engine. It came alongside and once more closed. They were now near to the next corner and because this was again a left-hander, the Land-Cruiser had only to keep pace with them to cut them off. His obvious move was again suddenly to brake and to try to come round the rear of the other vehicle. He braked for a split second, then floored the accelerator. The driver of the Land-Cruiser matched their braking, but was caught out when they accelerated. Unfortunately, they were up to the corner. He used opposite lock to set up the car, then steered into the corner. He almost made it, might have done had the surface of the road not been covered with gravel-like detritus. The tyres failed to hold their grip and momentum took them over the edge.

He wasn't aware of any sickening sense of catastrophe, of wondering how far they had to fall and whether they would be crushed inside the shattered car. His mind experienced only a blur of motion and helplessness which ended with a violent force that sent him straining against the seat-belt and a burst of ugly sound.

The world slowly returned into sharp focus. He found the car was right side up, tilting sharply forward. He stared through the shattered windscreen. The bonnet, badly buckled, had slammed into a cork tree which had not recently been harvested so that its thick, puffy bark had acted as a buffer. But for that tree, they would have landed several metres lower, on boulders. His door had sprung and was wide open. There was a smell of petrol.

He looked to his right. Aznar did not appear to have been injured, but he was motionless and his gaze was fixed. 'Get out,' Brent shouted, trying to break through the shock that was clearly gripping the other. Aznar said nothing and did nothing. Brent released his own safety-belt, then Aznar's. He reached across and tried to open the far door, but it refused to move. He scrambled out, gained as firm a foothold as he could, reached inside and grabbed hold of Aznar's shirt.

There was a whoosh of sound as the leaking petrol caught fire. Brent shouted in four-letter English as he pulled and either the language or a sudden realization of the danger he was in brought Aznar to his senses; he scrambled out of the car.

They reached a safe distance, then turned and stared at the burning car. Aznar began to tremble so hard it was as if he had the ague.

In the hotel bedroom Brent poured himself out another brandy from the bottle he had earlier bought at a supermarket. He returned to the balcony and sat on the cane chair, stared out at the sea and the several sail–boards whose patterned sails added bright splashes of colour to the scene.

He drank, enjoying the extra pleasure that came from knowing that he was lucky to be alive and able to do so. The car-hire firm had seemed remarkably undisturbed by the news that the Fiesta was a write-off and had accepted without question his and Aznar's evidence that the driver of the Land-Cruiser must have been so drunk that he had not known what he was doing; so undisturbed that he wondered if perhaps they were more than content to have one of their cars replaced by the insurance company. Thankfully, the police had been equally uninquisitive. Since neither he nor Aznar were able to give the registration number of the Land-Cruiser, there was virtually no chance of tracing it and—so their attitude had suggested—who was going to worry too much over yet one more accident involving a foreigner?

Capllonch's family had obviously been kept under observation by a couple of members of the local drugs mob whose job was to make certain they remained too scared to tell authority anything; Capllonch's son had told them the name of the foreign visitor who was asking questions about his father and they had identified the Englishman as one of the two detectives who had been pressuring Hawsley back in England; with mistaken stupidity, instead of finding out what to do, they had acted on their own initiative and had decided to eliminate the inquisitive English detective. Mistaken stupidity because by their murderous action they had confirmed as fact what until then had been only supposition.

But if they had confirmed, they had not provided proof. He was no nearer being able to prove than he had been before. And his failure must have placed Susan in even greater danger . . .

He drained the glass. He swore. He returned to the room to pour himself another drink. And then, as he held the bottle poised over the glass, it suddenly came to him that if he were prepared to betray his principles—a small price to pay for Susan's safety—it was this failure which offered him the chance to succeed.

CHAPTER 22

Brent parked in front of the garage at Cockscomb Farm, walked down to the garden and around the house to the front door. He rang the bell.

Caroline Hawsley opened the door, her expression matching the vinegary tone of her voice. 'What do you want now?'

'I'd like a word with Mr Hawsley.'

'Anything more you have to say can be said to our solicitors.'

'I'm certain he'd rather I spoke directly to him.'

'What do you mean by that?'

'That it is very much in his interests.'

She stared at him, clearly wanting to bring an abrupt end to the conversation, yet experiencing too much doubt to do so. Finally, she moved to one side. He entered the hall. 'Ashley,' she called out.

After a moment Hawsley appeared on the small landing.

'The detective says he wants to speak to you and claims it's in your interests.'

'Why?'

Neither she nor Brent answered. He came down the stairs and as he stepped on to the floor, she led the way into the sitting-room. She sat down on one of the armchairs. 'Now, perhaps you'll explain just what this is all about?'

Brent had not been asked to sit, but he sat and made himself comfortable. 'It starts with the day the Sergeant found the crack in Mr Hawsley's coat pocket.'

'That is a wicked lie,' she said angrily.

'That's right, it is.'

They stared at him, utterly confused by the admission.

'He was planting it to try and pressure Mr Hawsley into telling the truth about Maureen. But what I'm suggesting now is that you tell the truth and admit that you weren't in the house at the time and that your husband lies and says that he was in possession of the crack.'

'You must be mad! This is utterly ridiculous! I shall inform our solicitors—'

'I wouldn't if I were you. Because if you do, I shall have to pass on the details of my visit to the Rotga Winery and what happened when I wanted to have a chat with Joan Capllonch.'

'I have not the slightest idea what you're talking about.'

'But your husband has.'

She swung round. The expression on Hawsley's face was unmistakably one of fear.

'This has been a case,' continued Brent, in a quiet, even

voice, 'in which the truth has become lies and lies have become truth.

'The Rotga Winery is a legitimate wine-making and exporting company which fronts for an illegal trade in drugs; the Seetonhurst Wine Company is a legitimate importer of wines, fronting for the illegal importation of drugs. Capllonch, an employee of the winery, worked for both the legitimate and the illegitimate sides of the business. A greedy man, he wasn't content with the extra money he was making, but wanted much more, so he began stealing small quantities of drugs and selling these on his own account.

'Your husband is employed as an accountant for both the legitimate and the illegal financial affairs of the Seetonhurst Wine Company. In the second role he has made frequent visits to Spain and during one of these he discovered that Capllonch was thieving. Like him, your husband was not content with what he was getting, but wanted more, and he forced Capllonch to enter a partnership and to increase the size of the thefts. It was a highly profitable partnership up to the time when Capllonch betrayed himself or was betrayed, and in consequence was murdered. Luckily for your husband, his part in the theft was not uncovered; had it been, he also would have been murdered.'

She made a sound that was like a low moan of pain. Then she clasped her hands together and rested them on her lap and stared into the far distance. She had taken the only escape route left to her.

'You can't prove anything,' Hawsley shouted wildly.

'That's right. But that's no reason to prevent you admitting everything and, in order to undo a little of the hellish damage you've helped cause, giving the police as much information regarding the mechanics of this trade as you can.'

'No.'

'You've really no sensible alternative. Do all you can to help and I'll forget what I know about Maggie and that

very expensive flat in Winslow Mansions; refuse and I'll
feed the news to the people in charge. It'll take them no
time at all to work out that you were in cahoots with
Capllonch. Any life insurances you hold will mature very
quickly.'

'You're . . . you're blackmailing me.'

'I suppose that in one sense I am. But compared to
murder and drug-dealing, I'd say that my crime is, like the
housemaid's baby, only a little one.'

Detective-Inspector Fawcus, in a rare display of open
anger, thumped his desk. 'Goddamnit, I told you to stay in
touch.'

'I'm sorry, sir,' said Brent. 'But I had to make a quick
trip to Spain.'

For a moment the DI was nonplussed. Then he regained
his composure. 'It seems you're quite incapable of understanding that rules and orders are to be obeyed. Or of
appreciating that your feckless behaviour hardly helps you
in respect of the coming inquiry into your and Sergeant
O'Connor's attempt to plant evidence on Mr Hawsley.'

'It sounds as if you're rather pre-judging us.'

The DI became tight-lipped. 'Very well, if that's your
response . . . The date of the hearing has been fixed for the
fourth of August. You will attend county headquarters at
ten in the morning. You are entitled to be legally represented. Have I made myself clear?'

'Very clear, sir. But what you've said does raise one point.
Will the hearing go ahead now that Mr Hawsley admits he
was in possession of the drug and Mrs Hawsley admits she
was not present until after the sachet was found?'

The DI was silent for several seconds, then he said: 'He's
prepared to lie—even though it will be so much to his own
detriment?'

'I think one should say that he is finally prepared to tell
the truth.'

'Will you explain why he should falsely admit to having committed a crime?'

'I'm not certain what's changed his mind.'

'Really? . . . I don't suppose you'd like to explain how you've worked it?'

'Worked what, sir?'

'Quite! Perhaps I'll sleep sounder if I don't know.'

Mrs Weston let Brent into the house. She said that Miss Susan was out, but Mrs Radford was in the lavender garden. He went through the house and out by the service door. In front of the gazebo was a small circular lawn ringed by a lavender hedge, and Veronica was kneeling on a rubber mat, weeding a small bed in the centre of it.

She settled back on her heels. 'Hullo, Jim. How are you?'

He said he was fine and was newly back from Spain where he'd bought her a small memento. She looked vaguely worried. As he handed her the bag, he guessed she was afraid that he was giving her a wooden Don Quixote. When she discovered it was a bottle, she relaxed and thanked him.

He indicated the wrapped box of chocolates in his left hand. 'These are for Susan. Have you any idea when she'll be back?'

'Not really.'

'Then will it be all right if I hang on a bit to see if she returns before long?'

'She certainly won't be back today.'

'Not? But I thought she was helping you look after two elderly relatives?'

'Good Heavens, no!'

'Then where is she?'

'Up in Derbyshire; at least, I think that's where she is.' Veronica came to her feet. 'Such a nice family. And Marcus is doing really well in the City.'

'Marcus?'

'He's their only son. It's so nice to see a son carrying on

the family traditions and preparing himself to inherit the estate.'

'D'you think she'll be staying there for some time?'

'It's quite likely, since they keep a good stable. But I really don't know. These days children do just as they wish, without any reference to their parents.'

Like temporarily shacking up with a detective-constable? 'I guess there's no point in my hanging on, then. Perhaps you'll give her these chocolates when she comes back—if they haven't become stale by then?'

He said goodbye and left.

Pam O'Connor said: 'He's in the front room . . . Since he heard when the hearing's going to be, he won't do anything but sit and watch the telly. I can't even get him down to the pub and you know how he used to like his pint.' Her lips trembled.

Brent spoke confidently. 'After I've had a word with him, love, we'll all be going to the pub for several pints.'

She looked up at him. 'You're not saying . . . You don't mean . . .'

'There'll be no hearing. Hawsley's admitting possession.'

She began to cry.

'Here, what's all this? That's supposed to be good news, not bad.'

'I can't help it. Don't you understand the first thing about women?'

'Probably not,' he answered, as he crossed to the door of the front room.